The Folk and Their Fauna

Amanda

Best Wishes

Scott D. Gottschalk

The Folk and Their Fauna

The Story of One Man's Love Affair with Animals

Scott D. Gottschalk

To order additional copies of this book, contact:
Xlibris Corporation
1-888-795-4274
www.Xlibris.com
Orders@Xlibris.com
89857

CONTENTS

ALSO BY SCOTT D. GOTTSCHALK

Nine Lives To Eternity

A True Story of Repeatedly Cheating Death
An Inspirational and Faith-driven Human Triumph

All praise and honor to our God in his glory,
for His will shall be done thus never to worry.
You can make the world a better place for all,
so simply stop taking up space before the fall.
Express life with a bountiful joy and a zest;
nine lives to eternity reflects our Lord is best.

—Scott D. Gottschalk (2010)

With love to Dad and Mom, Julie, Jerry, Sally, and Marcia, because of whose undying family love, I had a foundation on which to write this book, and to my wife, Astrid, for her understanding and her support in helping me complete my task

All the animals we cherish and love,
God made the folk and their fauna from high up above.
He bade we should share with each other united,
To keep a world that will remain undivided.
Man and beast working side by side,
'Til the end of all time we shall always abide.

—Scott D. Gottschalk

1

○ ○ ○ ○

Remember the First

Everyone has memories at one time or another of an intriguing moment with an animal, whether they be exciting or sad. The farm where I grew up is a virtual menagerie of creatures that come in all sizes and shapes. Here on the farm, animals are born, grow with time, and eventually die, as everything progresses. In most instances, however, their death does not take part before a unique experience has evolved. These creatures leave behind a part of themselves, if only in the form of a memory that can be forever cherished and remembered as we grow older.

Remember the first if you can. Was it a puppy, a cat, or possibly a horse? Think way back to the very depths of your memory to that first animal experience. Sure, in some cases, it may not have been pleasant. By remembering the first, you may rekindle the thoughts of anguish from being bitten in the leg by a dog or thrown from a horse. When the truth is on the line, though, I'll bet the total animal experiences were positive.

Although not all of the stories in this book of my animal experiences relate to farm animals, most do tie in with the farm background that I grew up in. I will cover an array of the animal kingdom I've associated with, and I hope you will have had some contact with a member of the mammalian, avian, or reptilian species, or possibly some other form of fauna I'll be talking about. The times I've shared with different animals have probably been in no way unprecedented by many of your own experiences. One common factor of human nature that we all share is our love of making conversation about the animals in our lives. We humans often talk so often about animals; they're second only to the weather as a conversation topic. Each and every one of us has, at one time or another, done a little bragging about how my dog could retrieve at three months of age or how your calf won the state grand championship. It's second nature to us, and the enjoyable part is we can brag and carry on about something other than ourselves, and yet we take all the glory of the achievements won by our nonhuman friends. Remember your first, if you will, as I share my first with you.

My life began on a farm in southern Minnesota, near a small rural town called Hammond. On this quaint little farm, the first of many fond memories began to emerge, and, as I grew from a small and curious boy into a young man, the realization of God's place for animals began to take hold in my mind.

Dad always took a special interest with my sister and me to see that we respected the beauty of some animals, the awesome size characteristic of a few, and the fragility of still others. My sister Julie, who was three, and I, at age five, often spent hours viewing the habits of our farm animals. Dad had a small beef herd with a monstrous, horned Hereford bull. Each day Julie and I would get a little braver, and time after time Dad would say, "You kids stay away from the bull! They don't always mean harm, but a bull doesn't always know how strong he really is, and he should never be trusted." Embedded in my memory was the image of the bull's gargantuan set of horns and his red, beady little eyes as he lumbered past me while I sat on the wooden fence. Many times I would go exploring out in the pasture (unknown to my parents, of course), and it was like a risky and highly exciting game to see if I could get from point to point without drawing the attention of the bull. It's almost disappointing now to look back at pictures of the bull and face the fact that what once appeared to be a huge omnipotent beast was in reality a quite scrawny and not-so-enormous bull.

In those early days of my life, it was not uncommon to be brought up on a farm. It often amazed me when friends or relatives from the city would come to visit us and would act apprehensive about our dog, Rex. Rex was a well-mannered bundle of tail-wagging joy. He was a fine-quality, highly bred canine with everything from collie to terrier for ancestry. Rex, like most farm dogs, let loose a vocal tirade on any car that would chance to come into the driveway. For a dog he really wasn't good for anything but barking. He didn't chase sticks, herd cattle, or even do a good job of being a watchdog, but old Rex was the first four-legged, hairy-bodied creature I remember, and even though it's been years since I've heard his bark, the memory still lingers of that faithful farm dog's obedient look and the desire to please in his eyes.

Dad and Mom had all the critters it took to make a complete farm for a couple of growing children. On one end of the yard were a few pigs with a corncrib in front of their pen. It was always fun to pass the pigpen and listen to them grunting and begging for more food. In another building was the sheep headquarters. There were only two sheep, and it was their duty to keep the grass cropped down in the ditches and among the trees. Seldom did one ever see the sheep with their heads up. The whole day was spent taking luscious wisps of green grass and chewing them down with the quick, tight, chewing fashion of a sheep. Naturally, there was the chicken house. No farm can be complete without chickens. Not only were we so lucky as to have a small chicken house with about fifty white chickens, but there were also bantam chickens running around outside.

Bantam chickens are a small and beautifully colored fowl. They lay little brown eggs, which, if not collected, would soon become flocks of little chicks running all over. The roosters could often be found sitting proudly in a tree with their chests thrust forward. Bright and early in the morning they would begin strutting about as though nothing but them mattered. They would let everyone within miles know that the sun had just come up and it was time to start the day. They did this in their own personalized form of an ear-splitting crow. Usually the cocky little roosters had their own territories marked and normally stayed within the boundaries, but, as nature will often have it, one rooster would surmise that the hens of the other rooster's harem were more alluring, or whatever passes through the mind of a lovelorn, mating rooster. Before long, the colored feathers would begin to fly as a full-fledged chicken fight started.

A chicken fight is as much fun to watch as a heavyweight boxing match (if that's one's game). It is an amazing sight to see hens, sheep, cats, pigs, and cattle all watching the "battle of champions." Sometimes the loser would have to "fly the coop," as they say, and other times the bereaved battler was severely or fatally injured. It was at times like this that the family had a chicken feast for supper.

The last of my favorite childhood experiences on this farm was with an old cat that had been given to our family by a neighbor. It seemed that every time one saw her, she was walking around with a new litter of kittens. For this reason my sister and I thought up the strikingly original name of Mother Cat and so christened her. She was an avid hunter, who could often be seen miles from home stalking through ditches or walking fields in quest of a tasty rodent for lunch. Once my father and I witnessed a most incredible example of instinct versus instinct. The old chicken house had been empty for quite some time, and one day we decided to clean it out. The one detail I vividly remember is, as Dad opened the door and looked in, he said excitedly, "Quick, Scott, go get Mother Cat. There are two huge rats in there." Swift as a light, I flew off, calling, "Here kitty, kitty, here, kitty, kitty." It is appropriate to explain, however, that no matter how well kept up a farm is or how many cats there are (thanks to Mother Cat, there were many by this time), rats somehow can find ways to propagate themselves. They can live in hay, straw, under buildings, in walls, or anyplace else that will accommodate them. Not too often did one get a chance to see a rat in broad daylight, but, when one was spotted, the normal farmer will call in his most powerful defense. In our case it was Mother Cat.

In no time at all, I had her in my small arms and was traveling at breakneck speed to get back to the chicken-house before the rats decided there were better ways to spend the afternoon. As soon as I came huffing and puffing up to the building, Dad seized the cat from my arms, flung open the door, and threw her at the foe. Everything from here on in happened in a flash. Mother Cat, being a very adept killer in such instances, knew she could get only one of the rats, so, before we could comprehend what was happening, one of the rats came steaming right for the doorway.

Now I've seen my father do some relatively phenomenal feats in his life, and there is a little he is afraid of, but there can be no mistake of his fear when it comes to rats. Dad yelled, "Look out!" and, the next thing I knew, he was trampling over my little body to escape the wrath of the oncoming rat. Naturally, the only objective in the rat's mind was to escape, and, as soon as he cleared the doorway, he was gone from sight. As soon as the danger was over, we ran back to see what Mother Cat was up to. She had the big rat backed into the far corner and was cautiously proceeding forward.

It is a well-known fact in rural areas that a rat will run until cornered, and then it will fight ferociously for its very existence.

Mother Cat was beginning to get second thoughts, so Dad yelled, "Get 'im, Mother Cat!" I, of course, was chiding with my high-pitched and somewhat excited voice to get him too. All of a sudden the rat lunged at the cat. As if suddenly realizing this hairy, slithery, creepy creature was almost too much of a match, she flipped over on her back and brought the rat directly above her with her four paws holding him tightly. The rat was squeaking horribly, and the cat was tenaciously snarling up a storm. Then, in one continuous motion, she reached up with her teeth, grabbed the rat by the throat, turned back to her feet, and then shook her head spastically from side to side. In moments, the rat lay limp in her mouth, and Mother Cat triumphantly strode off with a hard-earned meal for her latest litter of hungry mouths.

This friendly old cat has always been remembered by my family for her fertile tendencies and hunting abilities, which extended far beyond the call of duty.

With the coming of fall in that sixth year of my life, my mother made a decision that drastically changed the lives of everyone in my family. I was of school age, but the only available institution was a little, one-room schoolhouse for all grades, one through eight, just down the road. Mom made the decision that the farm and all the animals would have to be sold to make way for my education. Dad sadly agreed after many hours of deliberation, and, before long, the farm was sold.

To this day, I still remember my father's long face when the auction sale was held. Although my father is a stalwart individual, I think I might have caught a glimpse of a tear or two stream from his eyes as he took his last look at the farm, ironically from the very fence my sister and I used to observe the animals.

Dad's dearly prized tractor and all the animals he had loved, fed, and cared for so well, for so long were suddenly going off to different parts of the country with new owners. Eventually the farm was bare and silent. We loaded up our household goods and moved to the city.

We made our new home in the city of Rochester, Minnesota, where I started my first year of school. At times, in the back of my young mind, though, I could still hear the pigs grunting, the chickens clucking, and the cattle mooing out in the yard of our old farm. At night I would come home, and there were no chores to do. Dad hated to sit around and watch television, but he couldn't find much to occupy his time. Julie and I fought all the time, and Mom was quite irritable. We all wished we could have returned to the life that had once made us so happy.

2

○ ○ ○ ○

Unmistakably Man's Best Friend

With my family being urban dwellers at this time, this point in our lives could easily have been the end of my story. My little clan could compliantly have settled down and adjusted to a life within the city, a life just like what so many other agricultural families had adjusted to in the past and would continue to adjust to in the future. Yes, my father could have adjusted to the routine of going to work in the morning, then coming home at night. He could have decided on settling down to television after supper or spending an evening playing cards with the men. My mother could have eventually learned to enjoy her many carefree hours in the house. For once in her life, she was able to relax and spend some time during the day doing things that meant something to her. Now there was no responsibility of having to go out to do chores, no threat of her clean floors getting dirtied by muddy boots. Even my sister and I might have become satisfied with going to school, then coming home and playing on the sidewalk by ourselves or with friends.

From what one has read of this not overly exciting chapter thus far, it's easy to see why the boring details of a life like this were a bit much for my family to cope with. A lifestyle that had once been filled with daily excitement was now a dragging affair, and there seemed nowhere to turn. If possible, however, bear with me, because a drastic change in plot is just around the corner.

For a farm family, adjusting to a new mode of life such as this can take years. My father gave it a few months—six months, to be precise.

In the six months of city living, much had happened to the family, and we realized our true feelings. Our most outstanding feeling was how terribly we missed our country lifestyle.

One joyous occurrence in this period was the birth of my new baby brother. We named him Jerry. When Dad brought Mom and Jerry home, it was such a new experience that everyone forgot about his or her misery for the time being. Jerry was a fat, red-faced little devil that, like so many babies, was blessed with a powerful set of vocal cords. Julie and I played with him every chance we had. Dad would lie on the couch and jostle Jerry around. He would often toss him up in the air, then catch him again. With each toss, Jerry would break out into a new outburst of childish laughter. My Father always enjoyed this activity, at least until my brother spat up or burped in his face.

Everything went fine for a few months, but, as fate would have it, the family sank back into fresh depths of depression. After the novelty of Jerry's birth wore off, Dad kept repeating over and over again how he missed the animals, chores, and the clean, cool morning air just after the sun rose over the hill. I heard him tell Mom once how it made him awfully sad to think his new baby son was going to have to experience cows and horses on somebody else's farm.

To this day I thank the Lord for Dad's persistence in wanting the farm life back again, because one day Mom and Dad just up and said,

"We're moving back to the country." Needless to say, no one shed any tears that day.

On a fine weekend day in early fall, when the leaves on the trees were just turning colors and the field crops were beginning to lose their summery green, my family went for a little ride in our car. Our destination was a tiny rural town called Byron. Byron was barely a spot on the map and didn't have many businesses in town to speak of. Byron was so close to the larger city of Rochester, it didn't have a movie theater, a swimming pool, shopping centers, or many other normal community affairs usually associated with small towns. With its increased activities, I feel Byron still has the unique qualities of being more relaxed, slower paced, and friendlier than most cities.

Little towns like Byron are often sneered at and called hicksville or redneck centers. Towns such as this are rapidly heading for extinction, and no one can ever know the true meaning of growing up in a small town, unless he has first-hand experience.

Dad first directed the car onto a bumpy blacktop road going south from Byron and then onto an old gravel road going west. Lo and behold, before our all-inquisitive eyes was our new farm. It was a little sixty-acre patch with just about all one could hope for. In the rolling pasture was a meandering creek that just set me to twitching all over for the want of exploring it. Big, beautiful oak and evergreen trees were all around, ideal for tree houses. There was a barn with a big hayloft and an upright, circular, cement silo right next to it. The farmhouse, not the most modern facility, lacked running water, electricity, and central heating. Alongside the house was an old wooden outhouse. Since the old house was nearly a hundred years old, it was decided that it should be completely renovated before we took up residency there.

The former house in the city was sold, and the family temporarily moved into an apartment in Byron until the farm was ready for occupancy. Every morning, Julie and I walked to our new school, where we soon formed friendships that lasted the rest of our schooldays. Each day Mom and Dad would work for hours alongside the carpenters, electricians, and plumbers to prepare our new home. One weekend several weeks later, my family made its final move back to the farmland and rural life we had desired for so long.

It was because of this move I was able to spend my lifetime with some extremely special animals that possessed a few of the unusual personalities that make up my book. This story is about the first animal to set foot on the new farm property.

Naturally, no farm is complete without its dog, and thus I will share with you a story about a most delightful little creature that spent more years of her life with my family than did any other single animal. She shared so many experiences with us in her existence that one chapter of a book could never cover the joy she could radiate, the pleasure she could bring.

One day after the family was getting good and used to the idea of the fresh country air, the friendly rural folks, and the beautiful view from our window each morning, my father stated, "Well, kids, do you think it's about time we get some animals around this property?" I can assure you, we were not hesitant in answering, "Ya, ya, ya."

That morning Dad secretly went to see a friend of his on the other side of town. There he picked out a puppy from a litter that was just being weaned. I'm sure that, had my sister and I known of my Father's intentions, we surely would never have been able to board the orange school bus and ride to our institution of learning on that morning. As it was, Dad brought the little black-and-white puppy home. There, he put her in a box out in the barn to await our arrival later in the day.

That afternoon, Julie and I got off the bus in much the same manner as we had gotten on, then proceeded to walk up the driveway to the house. Once we were in the house, it didn't take much arithmetic on our part to figure out something was up. It wasn't every day we came home from school to find both parents sitting at the table smirking at us. Of course, my little brother, Jerry, had already been let in on the secret, but, being only age one, he hadn't shown much more interest than a single tug on the puppy's ear and then total disenchantment. My sister and I, however, were about to burst with overwhelming curiosity because of the peculiar actions of our parents. Luckily, though, my father had never been a person to keep one in suspense long, and he immediately said, "You kids just might want to check that old barn out. Mom and I have been hearing an awful lot of commotion going on out there all day. Almost sounds like yipping or barking possibly."

At that point, if our Dad had said anything else, we surely didn't hear it, because we were already halfway to the barn in an all-out run. Julie was almost in a frenzy yelling, "Scott! Slow down so we can see it together." I, of course, was retaliating by screaming back, "Why don't you hurry up, you old slowpoke!" I reached the barn door first, flung it open, and thrust myself forward. Right behind came Julie, almost stepping on my heels. With our hearts pounding in our ears and each of us gasping for breath, we looked for the first time at the puppy. Little did we know she was a puppy who would grow up with us and surprisingly still be alive when we became young adults.

If Dad and Mom had not been smart enough to follow us down to the barn, we just might possibly have mauled the puppy to death with our loving hands. We immediately wanted to know what kind of dog she was, and Dad replied simply "She's a fox terrier." Later we were told that fox terriers were so named, because they were taken out hunting for foxes as well as other large burrowing animals. Because of their small size, they were sent in the holes after the animals.

Dad gave us the task of naming the puppy, and we faced the challenge. I yelled out the old standbys, "Spot, Rover, or Butch." Mom reminded me that it was a female puppy. Julie jumped at her chance by yelling, "Lady, Mary, and Queen." Dad wasn't overly impressed by any of our brainstorms and told us, "Think about a name for a few days. Maybe the puppy's actions or habits will give you some ideas." It was just as well, because we were in too much ecstasy to think properly anyway.

We had only been playing with her for about fifteen minutes and just getting to know her when Dad said, "Okay, kids, let's go back to the house now. She's had a rough day by getting separated from her mother, brothers, and sisters. She also has a whole new human family to become accustomed to. If we get her any more excited, she could get sick." Reluctantly, along with several sighs and moans of dissatisfaction, we retreated to the boring house, where there wasn't anything to do.

During the next two hours, my sister and I made life miserable for Mom. Every ten minutes like clockwork we would pester her to let us go see the puppy. Finally, at about five-thirty, just before supper, she gave us some warm milk and food to take out to the puppy. O joyous occasion!

Quick as a wink we were with our little black-and-white friend again, watching her gobble and slurp the food. Once in a while she would sneeze, whenever, by chance, she'd get some liquid down her cold little black nose. Again, Dad forced us to cut the reunion short, so we stalked back to the house, pouting. I distinctly remember that nearly sleepless night, as I pondered about the puppy. I wondered if she was all right, and I longed to be playing with her.

Each day Dad would let us play with her just a little longer, and soon it wasn't long before she was allowed to romp from the barn.

We laughed so hard while watching her try to run with her oversized, pudgy body and little tiny legs that could barely get her belly off the ground. It didn't take long for the little dog to begin looking for us and longing for our touch.

Not so long after we got the little terrier, she began to pick up a habit she carried with her to the end of her days. Her favorite spot to be stroked and petted was her belly. Whenever anyone would reach down to pet her, she would flop right over on her back with feet sticking straight out and expect to be catered to. She would almost look you right in the eye as if to say, "Come on, what are you waiting for. What's the difference if you pat my head or my belly?" It then stood to reason, when I chose Tippy as her name, everyone gladly agreed there could be no better appellation.

Tippy grew unbelievably throughout that last half of our first winter on the farm. The next spring, almost unknowingly, she had grown into a beautiful, sleek dog that could run like the wind and was truly a sight and joy to behold.

With the coming of spring, all the members of our family knew that, before long, Tippy would no longer be the sole animal to have the run of the farm. Dad was getting extremely anxious for some chores. He wanted to put some cattle in the pasture along with some more chickens, pigs, and cats to populate the barnyard.

My father's next major investment for the farm came in the form of a small herd of dairy cows. He had been working diligently for the past few weeks preparing the farm for the cattle. Hay and straw had been placed in the loft of the barn. The barn had been painted both inside and out with the not-too-colorful, but sanitary-looking color of white. A quaint little milk room was built to house the milking equipment and store the milk. The stalls and stanchions of the barn were fixed up to provide a comfortable home for the cows. Last, my father and I walked the pasture to fix the dilapidated fence surrounding it, and I assure you there was a lot to be fixed.

As soon as my father finished with the fencing, he unloaded his newly purchased cows on the farm to meet with everyone's approval. Of course, the family was elated at the new livestock, but anyone or anything that felt he could become a part of that farm without Tippy's consent had another "think" coming.

Once the cattle were in the barnyard, she set right to barking and fussing up a storm. I could almost read her thoughts as she was probably thinking, "How dare they set foot on my territory." It was quite comical to watch her go barking and running after a large cow. It was, however, short-lived as my father yelled, "Tippy, get away from there." As always, Tippy had to go through the "crushed feeling" routine that was unique to her. Immediately, the tail went between the legs, ears went from upright to flat beside her head, and her head was placed in the sunken, pouting position. Then with sad, hurt eyes, she would beg forgiveness. Without exception, she always got it. In minutes, everyone was happy again, especially Tippy.

Tippy gladly gave up her large, spacious barn she had used for her quarters. The cows definitely needed the space more than she did. Her new residence was still in the barn, but now it was a box in the corner. Her box was positioned just to her liking, so at any given time of the day she could view all the action taking place.

Tippy always seemed to enjoy the presence of other animals, and I loved to watch her habits around them. One favorite trick of hers was to go down the front of the cows while they had their heads in the stanchions. With quick, darting motions, she would reach out, lick the startled cow on the snout, then proceed to the next cow. If one were to see this from the rear of the cows, it would look funny to see a whole line of cows go through the domino effect, the first cow backing up, the second, and so on, until the last cow in the line was reached.

One of Tippy's relatively famous attributes was her love and envy of horses. When I say "famous" I am referring to her reputation among the townspeople and rural neighbors who had seen and known about her peculiar actions around horses. At this point, however, I will reserve the right to hold you in suspense and tell about this part of Tippy's life in later chapters dealing with the ponies and horses I've associated with.

It was the special little traits Tippy had that gained her so much love from all my family members. One enjoyable part of the day was to watch her conflicts with the birds in the trees. It was a personal battle she had taken on when she was still a mere pup. To her, there was no distinction between "bad birds," such as crows, and good birds such as robins and bluebirds. Likewise, it made little difference whether the birds were starlings or sparrows. To Tippy, any bird that landed in her masters' trees was definitely trespassing. She would sit by the hour with as many trees as possible under her surveillance. When per chance a bird would land in a tree, Tippy would immediately begin her attack. She would bark, growl, yip, and whine. Around and around the tree she would circle. In most cases, the birds paid her little attention because of their high vantage point. This often proved to be their mistake. Tippy would start jumping up and down. If the bird still didn't get riled, this spurred her on to even higher fits of rage. Sometimes she would take a long run at the tree and jump right up into the crotch of it—providing the crotch was not too high. Not only would the noise of the leaves rustling help to rid the tree of the bird, but the slight movement of the branches caused by the dog's impact was usually the determining factor. Off the bird would fly, and, with a renewed sense of accomplishment, Tippy would jump down from the tree and go back to her surveillance point.

When Tippy was younger, all the family members would try to discourage the little terrier from this ridiculous habit. Every time she made an attempt on a bird, we would severely reprimand her. My father was not pleased by the prospect of a yard full of trees bare of birds. For some reason though, this was one trait of Tippy's that was not discourageable. Evidently she must have thought, "No matter what the punishment, I'll have to carry on this crusade for the advantage of my masters." It was a battle, though, that she would never win. In later years, as she got much older, the birds would land, and all she could muster up was a subtle bark and a dirty look. All the acrobatics she had performed in her earlier years were to be just history.

Another of Tippy's personable peculiarities was her ability to smile. Now this may seem to be absurd to many people. Who ever heard of a smiling dog? Well, it is possible, and Tippy was not a rare case in this instance. I have actually witnessed other dogs that could do this trick. When she was extremely happy she could give a smile unparalleled by anyone.

Her favorite smiling time, which of course was directly proportional with her happiness, occurred when the family came home after being away for a while. The amount of time we were gone usually made little difference to her, just so long as we had returned. Everyone would pile out of the car and start lavishly to smother her with attention. Almost before the car door could open, Tippy would curl up those lips and just be grinning away. It is unnecessary to mention that, at times like this, her old tail would almost be wagging itself right off.

A smile from one human to another can be a sign of friendship, love, and affection. I can assure you that a smile from this little dog was all inclusive of the same signs as a smile from another human being.

Tippy's most notorious addiction was her love of tractors. It may have been a mistake, but, when she was just old enough to get around rather freely, my father allowed her to tag along with him into the field while he did his field work. It soon got to be such an exciting game for Tippy that, even when any of us kids would just sit in the seat of the tractor to play, she would start getting all excited, wagging her tail, and start barking.

Spring and fall are the main times of the year a farmer does his field work, which consists mainly of tillage of the soil, planting the crop, and harvesting the crop. With the coming of both seasons, Tippy would wait in utter anticipation for her chance to follow the tractor. Each day, while my father would go around and around the field, plowing or doing some other such job, Tippy could be seen walking in the furrow right in back of the piece of machinery being pulled by the tractor.

Normally the blackbirds chose days like this to fly in and feast on the freshly overturned earthworms that inhabited the soil. Yes, you guessed it. Tippy was constantly chasing after the birds. From practically sunup until sundown each day, until the field work was finished, she would circle that field with my father.

In the years to come, the farming operation expanded, and property was bought at various other locations. Some of our land was now three to four miles away. By this time I was old enough to drive a tractor. When Dad and I would drive out of the yard from the home farm with our tractors, Tippy would be following close behind. The tractors could go at a pace of about sixteen to eighteen miles per hour. It always amazed me how that little bundle of energy could run four miles at that pace, walk the field all day, chase birds, run home again at the same pace, and still be just as peppy as when she left home.

I realize now that it was probably the superb shape she maintained that allowed her to live for so many years. As Tippy did get older, my Dad would carry her on the tractor to the fields because he said he didn't want her to have a heart attack or something like that. Once in the field, he would let her down from the tractor to do all day what she enjoyed most.

My father loved that dog more than any other animal he had ever owned. He made sure she was always being taken care of and fed. When she got too old to brave the elements in our cold Minnesota winters, it was his decision to have her moved from the old barn that no longer had cattle in it up to the garage of our house. Tippy was a constant friend to him. When he went out all alone early in the morning, she was always by his side. In relationships such as these, no wonder it's acclaimed that a dog is a man's best friend.

On a given occasion, in her younger years, Tippy chose to be promiscuous. By this I mean she came "in season," or heat, at nature's calling, and soon every courting male dog in that part of the country had visited her. We all knew in the following weeks that the increasing dimension of her bloating belly was caused by something other than overeating on her part.

One morning, Tippy came to eat her daily meal just like any other day, except she looked different. She was skinny as a rail. Immediately a search was on, because we realized her puppies had finally been born. The family spent the rest of the morning frantically searching every nook and cranny of that farm but couldn't find a trace of the puppies. The whole time, Tippy followed us from building to building expressing little interest. Alas, we felt depressed since we hadn't turned up any new arrivals. Suddenly, Mom said, "Where did Tippy go?"

Dad spotted her just as she rounded the corner of an old shed by the barn. We ran to the building, but once there, could find no sign of the young mother or her offspring. All at once Dad said, "Did you hear that? There was a whimper coming from under this building." Mom ran to the house for a flashlight and when she returned Dad began looking under the building for the objects we sought to find. He said at last, "Well, kids, I found Tippy, and she has her puppies under there." We were all excited and happy. Even my brother Jerry, who was beyond the baby stage now, showed some intrigue, although excitement has never been a strong characteristic in Jerry.

For some disgusting reason, Dad whispered something to Mom and then told us children we were ordered to the house until they had the puppies out from underneath the building. I was just about to give them my best argument when Dad cut me short and said, "Just take your brother and sister to the house. Don't give me any lip now." Well, who can argue with a terse statement like that? We huddled together and moaned our way back to the house.

The reason for Mom and Dad's strange actions we found out later when we were old enough to deal with what had happened. Tippy had used a hidden instinct that lies within the domestic dog, an instinct that seldom surfaces anymore. At one point in the dog's ancestry, it was a basic principle in nature to find the safest, most secluded spot to give birth. In this case, Tippy had chosen a spot under a building where it was much too cramped and airtight. Our parents had spared us the agony of watching them dig under the building and retrieving what they knew was there. Ten lovely little puppies had been born, but only three were barely alive.

Dad and Mom placed Tippy and the three remnants of her litter in a spacious, straw bedded corner of a building. Next, our parents quietly buried the rest of the litter. Not until all of this had taken place were we allowed to come and see the new arrivals. Mom and Dad never let on once what had happened, but, when I became a little older, Dad explained to me the details of that day.

Puppies are little creatures that young and old can never tire of. The three puppies were as different as night and day right from the start. One was solid black and, of course, called Blacky. Another was a goldish-tan color and was named Goldy. These two puppies, however, could never match up to the love and fun we shared with our favorite and third puppy. He was different from the beginning. Just a little bigger than the rest of his siblings, he was loose skinned and extremely sluggish. Clumsy was a word that much too lightly described him. I named him Dino, as in dinosaur, for obvious reasons. By some odd destiny, Dino just kept getting bigger and bigger. When he was born, he had paws practically the size of baseball gloves, and his head seemed almost as large as Tippy's.

One day my father inquired with the veterinarian about the possibility of Dino's having been sired by a neighbor's St. Bernard dog. The veterinarian explained a phenomenon called super fecundation. It occurs when a female dog ovulates; multiply releasing more than one egg to be fertilized. Although not extremely common, it is possible to have enough male dogs present at the proper time for fertilization of all the ovum to be accomplished by separate males. Obviously, in this case, Dino was one-half St. Bernard, and had a few phenotypic characteristics from his mother.

Poor Tippy and the other two puppies were so neglected by Julie, Jerry, and me that they began to become jealous.

The day came when the puppies were weaned and had to be given away. There was no way our parents could talk any of us into giving up Dino. We threatened to run away, stop eating, and even hold our breath until we turned blue. At last, giving in, our parents found fine homes for the other two puppies, and we were allowed to keep our favorite of favorites, Dino.

Unfortunately, I don't have much more to write about little Dino. He may have been a chapter in my book as was his mother, had it not been for a tragic accident. Even to this day, I think back to the details and the hurt still looms deep inside me.

It happened so quickly. Julie, along with Jerry, was swinging on the swing set, and I was playing with Dino. He still was very young and clumsy, but by this time was quite a bit larger than Tippy. Dino and I had already formed a lasting friendship in the short time he had lived on our farm. Nothing means more to a young boy than his own dog. Sure, there was Tippy, but she was a family dog. Naturally, Jerry and Julie liked to think Dino was theirs too, but he wasn't. Not in the same way at least. Dino and I would go exploring down by the creek in the pasture together or walk through the woods in back of the farm. I loved that dog, and what was about to happen next, I thought would rip me apart.

Mom had to go to town and do some shopping. She came out of the house, said goodbye to us, got in the car, and started backing out of the garage. It was at this very instant my Dino made his fatal mistake. Right under the rear tire of Mom's car he ran, and, needless to say, my mother ran over his little body. The worst of it was, I was right there. I heard him cry out and then total silence. Mom quickly shut off the car and got out. Julie and Jerry were running toward the car. What was I doing, one may ask. I was on my hands and knees, only a little, eight-year old boy with his dead dog under him, crying myself sick. Right now, as I write this and relive my memory of that day, I still get a little moist-eyed.

Mom felt terribly bad and said she would have Dad take care of him, but in my hysteria, I told her to get out of there and that I would bury him myself. To an outsider, the next sequence of events would surely have been a strange sight. Here we were, Julie carrying a shovel, Jerry carrying a hammer along with a small wooden cross I had just made, and I was carrying my dead dog. We were all walking along crying our eyes out as we marched out into one of my father's nearby fields. I chose a spot by a tree and dug a hole. Then, after placing Dino in and covering him up, I pounded the cross into the earth. Oh, how we bawled! I tried to say a prayer to God, but it was just a mass of blubbering. After staring at the grave for some time, we went back home. That night, I didn't sleep at all. Every time I stopped crying, I'd think of my little friend again and would start to cry all over again. Mom and Dad both came to my room and tried to comfort me.

As I remember it, my biggest dilemma was why my dog couldn't go up to heaven, although I could, someday. In church they were always saying that only people had souls. This really disturbed me, and I didn't understand how God could allow this. Those of us who come from a Christian background realize it is often a comforting thought to know that after death, there is something beyond to look forward to. In my case, I cared not for all the biblical gibberish dealing with human heavens. I just wanted to know what was going to happen to Dino now. Mom and Dad sat down on my bed and explained that God took into account all the animals that had died. They explained that, someday, when I went to heaven, Dino and I could be together again. As simply as that, I took what my parents had said for what it was worth, and for the time, my dilemma seemed not so magnified.

I'm sure that all people who have had a moving relationship with an animal can find some solitude in the fact that possibly there may be a time when one will be reunited forever with that special creature that made its lasting impression upon you.

As I explained in the beginning of this chapter, Tippy gave my family enough of herself to write a book on, rather than a mere chapter. However, in having touched on the highlights of her life, one can see that she was a most delightful little dog. A dog who had in her the desire to please and, as anyone who ever came in contact with her can vouch, did please.

Purposely I saved telling of Tippy's age until now. Sadly enough, as all things must come to pass, so did Tippy. She lived a most eventful life. Through her puppyhood and naming process, through the birth and death of some of her puppies, through cold winters, annoying birds, and joyous days in the fields doing field work, she lived and grew up with my family. Tippy became my friend when I was in first grade, just a child, and she was still my smiling little friend when I was a senior in college and living away from the farm. Yes, the sad time came when she was too old and too arthritic to chase birds or go with the tractor to the fields even though she tried. There came the day when my father sadly made her stay home from her beloved field. In her old age, she smiled less, her eyes looked so distant when one peered into them, and she seemed just too tired to tip over and be patted on her favorite spot.

Now, at better than sixteen years of age, our old family dog was about done. It's usually figured that one year in the life of a dog is equivalent to seven human years. This put Tippy, by our classification, at the more-than-ripe old age of one hundred and twelve years old, an amazing achievement, even for a sheltered dog.

Tippy first became deaf, and no amount of calling or whistling could grasp her attention. Next she began losing her sight. The last step in the process was her oncoming senility. Old Tippy would sit and bark at just about anything and at times nothing at all.

At last, one weekend I returned home from college to hear the heartbreaking news that Tippy was dying. Ironically, our everlasting friend was in the very spot in the old barn where, better than sixteen years earlier, she had frolicked as a puppy and brought so much happiness to my childhood. Mom and Dad thought she had suffered a stroke. She hadn't eaten or moved for two days. On top of all this, she knew no one in my family, including me. My father told me, "Scott, the old girl really broke me up when she went down. I went to the barn two days ago when this happened to say goodbye to her, and now I can't bear to see her anymore." I could hardly believe my ears. What an impact this little dog must have had on my father, to actually bring him to admit his sorrow and shed tears for her.

Everyone in my family knew that Tippy was suffering, but it hurt too much to think of having her put away. It's lucky that, while going to school I had been living away from the farm for some time, because I was strong enough to make my family understand her plight. I was unsure of whether or not she had suffered a stroke, but, in any case, Tippy had given up on living. If left there, she could linger on and suffer for days. Since she wouldn't eat and was surely bound to starve to death, I finally convinced my apprehensive family to go along with having her painlessly put to sleep.

The farm somehow seems different now that Tippy is no longer there. Oh, if you look really hard from a window, you sometimes might catch a glimpse of her jumping at a bird, or maybe the wind will play tricks and one can almost hear her excited bark as the tractors are started. The simple fact will always remain: Tippy was more than our best friend. To my family and that farm, she was larger than life.

3

o o o o

Not Always Loved by Many People

Snakes! Sounds like a creepy word to start out with, doesn't it? Even creepy, crawly snakes, however, are representative of some of the fauna on our earth. This tale is not one of your everyday, common pet stories. Usually, whenever snakes are involved, they will most likely arouse at least a casual interest in most folks, even if it is a fearful interest.

As one can probably tell, I am an avid animal-and creature-lover. My association with animals has never been confined just to a cat or possibly a dog. Not by any means have I ever been a person to bind my affection for animals to a limited number of species. People often like to consider themselves open minded, willing to try anything just once. Let me ask you: Were you ever open minded enough to try having a snake for a pet?

Oh, how Mom yelled at me. "Scott, for God sakes, what are you doing in this house with a snake?"

"But, Ma, I found him outside, and they make good pets," came my reply.

My mother's reaction was certainly not an uncommon one when a snake is involved, but I thought she was slightly overreacting. I mean why the big fuss? I hadn't walked into the house with an enormous, seven-foot-long boa constrictor wrapped around my neck and faking as though my eyes were being popped out of their sockets. All I had was a measly little garter snake, a modified, oversized angleworm. Sure, it had a long, flicking, forked tongue; little black, beady eyes; and lots of scales all over its body, but what made him so unattractive was certainly beyond me.

At close to the age of seven, I had just discovered a new play object. During one of my daily romps around the farm on an exploring expedition, I came across a swooshing sound accompanied by a rapid movement going through the grass. At first I thought it was a baby rabbit trying to escape from me, but when I finally caught up to the parting grass, I delightedly saw what was there. It was a colorful little garter snake or what is sometimes referred to, in error, as a grass snake. He was about a foot and a half long and certainly posed no great threat to me.

Even at my tender age, I had a pretty good working knowledge of snakes and a sort of hankering for them. When my mother used to take me to the library, I always had a strange liking for the books on snakes, dinosaurs, and whales. Without arguing, Mother would check out the books for me; then we'd go home, and she'd read them aloud to me. Peculiar as it may seem, I knew a fair amount of information about the species, even though I'd never seen a garter snake.

Here was a snake that was not poisonous, nor was he a constrictor with the ability to crush his prey. A garter snake doesn't even have teeth, but does have a rigid, hard, upper and lower set of gums. If provoked, he might strike out, and, as I was to find out later in life, can cause a minor gash with his jagged gums. These snakes have no great ability to harm man and, for the most part, serve as a great help. Garter snakes devour troublesome insects and rodents that often cause much damage to a farmer's crops. They hibernate underground in the winter and, like any other coldblooded creature, are dependent upon the external environment to sustain their body temperature. For this reason, snakes are sometimes seen sunbathing on a road or on bare rocks. I even knew that the garter snakes gave birth to live young, even though some species of snakes laid eggs.

Knowing all this about these particular snakes, I had no fear at the thought of picking him up. I carefully put my foot down on his slithering body, so as to halt his forward progress. I then reached down and, with my thumb and forefinger of one hand placed behind his head and my other hand under his body, I picked him up, just as the men in my library books had done. I wasted little time in running to the house to show Mom my new pet.

"Now, Scott, I don't care if they make good pets or not, you will not keep any snake in this house!"

"But, Mom, I'll keep him in a wooden box with a screen put over it."

My mother quickly snapped back, "Absolutely not, you keep that snake outdoors."

Boy, what a party-pooper. The thought of a snake in her cupboards or wrapped around her furniture was more than my mother could tolerate from me, I guess. At any rate, not to be defeated, I went outside, found a temporary can to put my new pet in, and proceeded to build the ideal home for him.

My father, being a farmer, had many kinds of livestock around his farm. Naturally, in order to keep the animals watered, he had to have livestock-watering tanks. I just happened to know where he had an extra one put away in a shed.

The rest of that day, I busied myself with getting the rather large, one-hundred-and-seventy-five-gallon watering tank out of storage and preparing it for its new occupant. Moving it was the most laborious task. The tank was about six feet long and three feet high. It was made of metal, which gave it a fair amount of weight, besides its obvious bulk. Being quite small, I spent a considerable amount of time, and sweat, before I pulled, grunted, and pushed the tank from the shed. I finally got the tank to the base of Dad's big silo. Here, I had it figured, was a protected spot from the wind, yet well positioned enough to absorb the rays of the sun, which was an important consideration for my little snake buddy.

That day, as I prepared the inside of the tank, I thought to myself, nothing but the best would do. First, I put some old boards under one end of the tank to make it slant downward. My next step was to get a hose and add water to the tank. The reason for the slant in the tank was so I could make a small pond in one end of the tank. This way my snake could swim and cool off.

Although garter snakes are usually found roaming the fields and pastures, they do need water. These snakes are exceptional swimmers and often live around a creek or pond. Here, they sometimes make their homes in cracks of rocks around the water and eat water insects.

To make a dry home and hiding place for him, I took my little red wagon and collected a stack of limestone rocks that were in my dad's pasture. Once back at the tank, I began piling them up in just the right manner inside the tank, so there were small crevices and caves, just perfect for a snake's hiding place. With that, my project was complete.

At once I added my snake to the tank. Much to my enjoyment, he first dived into the water, explored every inch of the far end of the tank, then came back and went directly under the rocks, where he remained for some time.

Choosing a name for my snake was an easy task. I spent little time deliberating about it. Before the day was out, I was already calling him "Mr. S."

Mr. S. could do nothing tricky or special. He certainly was not smart, as few reptilian species are, due to the minute size of their brains. He was spurred on by just basic instinct. When cold, he sunbathed; when hot, he took a swim; when hungry, he hunted.

My biggest chore was to satisfy his hunger. I would dig for earthworms whenever possible and add them to the tank. Mr. S. was always happy to oblige by devouring them. I also spent many spare moments going over every inch of Mom's house looking for flies that I could swat and therefore provide fresh protein for my pet.

Mom and Dad had put up quite an argument from the start about my keeping a snake as a pet. It was necessary, time and again, to prove he would do no harm to anything. Eventually, though, after seeing me set in my ways, they let me be. I suppose they realized that the snake was really no threat to me or the family, and it did give me some responsibility. Mr. S. by no means suffered from his captivity. I'm sure he had life much easier in his captive state than in the wild. Here was free food just for the taking, and he was quite protected from predators.

Many times I would take him from the tank and carry him to the lawn in our backyard for some exercise. I would set him down, and off he'd go, like a streak. I was always very careful not to let him get so far away that he could sneak off to freedom.

He was a young, immature snake when I first found him, extremely thin and small. Now, several months later, he was larger in girth and length. By now, he was close to his adult length of two and one-half feet. At the widest point in the middle, he had increased in diameter from about the width of one's little finger to about an inch and a half.

It was during the summer before first grade that I found Mr. S. It was now early fall, and I distinctly remember that first week of school when the teacher explained how our "show and tell" sessions would work. I could hardly sit still at the thought of bringing Mr. S. to school.

Well sure enough, the teacher gave me permission, and the following week I got my chance. On Monday morning I took Mr. S. and placed him in a rather large plastic container my mother had given me. I had put some grass clippings in the bottom, and added a few flies for food, and punched some holes in the top for air. That morning my mother drove me to school, for fear I would upset the school bus driver.

At last my opportunity arrived, and the teacher called on me to give my presentation for "show and tell." Boy, was I one proud little kid. I could hardly see because my chest was thrust out so far as I walked to the front of the class with my pet. Once up front, I gave all the information I had stored in my brain about snakes in general and especially my snake. Then I took off the cover and pulled Mr. S. out. To my surprise, almost every girl shrieked, and even Mrs. Wilson, my teacher, looked a little green. I can assure you, however, that all of the boys in my class were tingling with delight.

After the room had quieted down, my teacher asked if I would like to pick a friend and go around to the other classrooms to show them my pet. Obviously, the combination of being able to show off some more and getting out of class was too much to resist. I picked one of the boys, and off we trooped. I spent better than an hour that morning, knocking on classroom doors, explaining to each teacher what I had in mind, then giving my presentation. In each classroom it was the same; the girls screamed, and the boys roared their approval. Finally my "show and tell" was complete, and we returned to our classroom.

I set Mr. S. and his container in the back of the room, then sat in my seat for some absorption of knowledge.

That afternoon, after recess period, we came back from the playground to the classroom. I went to the rear of the room to check on Mr. S., and he was gone! The top of the container was askew, and a fresh outbreak of panic spread throughout the room. Not only were the girls, which included my teacher, in a hysterical state of mind, but most of the hotshot boys in the room were also a little less brave, now that a wily snake had just been unleashed.

Yes, somewhere in that room was my snake, and I had to find him. He would surely die in that school if left unattended. Not only was there no food available, but chances were he could go into a heat duct or something of the sort and perish for good. There was also the threat of my neck being wrung by a lot of frightened people, unless I found my pet soon.

At last, after scanning a major portion of the classroom, I found my friend. He was causing no trouble at all. His position, however, was not the most advantageous.

I'm sure most people have seen the paper cutters used in classrooms such as these. Usually, the teachers use them to cut construction paper for the pupils' art projects. The cutter consists of a flat board with a large, sharp-edged blade that pivots down to cut the paper. It was around this sharp blade that my snake had chosen to coil himself. His weight alone could have caused the blade to fall, and I might have had to take my snake home in about ten pieces.

I was quick to gather Mr. S. up, place him in the container, and cover it up again. Since it was only a short time before school was to let out, my teacher asked me to keep Mr. S. at my desk and make sure he stayed put.

At last, school was done for the day, and Mom picked me up again outside the school doors.

"How did 'show and tell' go?" she asked.

I said, "Mom, you'd never believe it."

After I had told her the whole story, she did not hesitate in telling me it would be a long time before I got that carried away for "show and tell" again.

Before long, another fall had come and almost gone. The colorful leaves were nearly gone from the trees now. Each day it seemed cooler and windier outside. Even the sun acted as though it just couldn't sneak out from behind the cloud cover. Knowing what I did about snakes, I realized I had to make a decision. With winter coming, I had two choices. I could either bring my pet in the house or let him go so he could find a place to hibernate for the winter.

I tried my parents first, but Mom was extremely vehement on her stand about snakes in her house. I pleaded with Dad to reason with her, but he backed her up completely.

Sadly, I was faced with letting my friend go. Now, how attached to a snake can one get, you might ask. Well, it's not exactly like losing a relative or having one's dog die, but I had developed a liking for Mr. S. Sure, he wasn't exactly the affectionate type, nor was he a purposeful type of pet. The point was, I had shared some good moments and laughs with him as he scared the girls; ate his flies, and wriggled through the grass for exercise.

At long last, I removed my pet snake from his private tank for the final time. I carried him to the spot where I had caught him and gently lowered Mr. S. to the ground. I was returning him to nature, and I was unafraid that he was too domesticated to fend for himself.

I was sure his instincts would act their part. As I watched him swoosh off through the dry, brown grass, I was glad that I had had yet another opportunity to share some time with one of God's creatures, a creature not always loved by many people.

4

○ ○ ○ ○

My Pony Paradise

"Dad, can't you understand? How many times do I have to tell you I want one bad?"

"If I were to allow you to get everything your heart desired, Scott, I would go broke."

The little discussion had started out as always. First, I would casually mention to my father or mother, how badly I wanted a pony. Then without the skip of a beat, either Mom or Dad would snap back about how a pony was too dangerous for a seven-year-old or how they ate more than they were worth.

Ever since I could remember, I had been fascinated by the equine species. When quite small, I used to beg Dad to buy me a ticket for a ride on the carrousel of ponies at the county fair. No stupid merry-go-round would suffice for this boy. I had to have the real animal. I would carry on and plead for rides like all children, when it came to a fair.

Like any normal parents, mine would often give in. Inevitably, I would be hoisted up on the pony's back. After all the children were in place, the ponies would start their endless trek around and around their captive circle. More times than not, I would get furious, because no amount of kicking or screaming would make the stubborn little ponies speed up their languid pace.

The owner of the pony ride would often reprimand me by saying "Son, can't you just sit tight like the other boys and girls?" I always wondered to myself, *What is it with this guy?* My idea of getting on a pony was not sitting like a "dead log" and clutching the saddle horn. No, my idea was to kick, spur, yell, slap, or do anything else to make the pony at least break into a fast walk.

When the walk was over, the man would go around and unload each pony of its burden. Invariably, it seemed I was somehow the first child off each time, and the man would be muttering something under his breath.

As I walked back to my family, Dad would say, "Was it fun, Scott?" and then quickly reply, "No, you may not ride again!"

I suppose my parents wished I would act more like Julie and Jerry at the fair. My sister and brother were content to beg for a ride on the play cars or the ferris wheel. When they had finished their rides, that was the end of it. With me, it was usually another matter, though. Each time I rode a pony at the fair, saw a horse along the road as we journeyed in the car, or saw a picture of a horse, I would besiege my parents with begging requests for a pony.

One of my best friends, who lived only a mile down the road, had owned ponies since the time he could walk. His name was Tom. I remember going to Tom's farm to play on sunny afternoons in the summer. We would spend some time in the hay loft, swinging from ropes or jumping in the loose hay. Next, we would go out in some thick bushes surrounding the yard and build a fort or play army. I can assure you, however, I never set foot on Tom's farm without getting to do a little pony riding.

One day, I was relentlessly attacking my folks on the usual matter of owning a pony. It must have at last dawned on them that my love of ponies and horses was authentic and not a simple whim. Dad told me he would try and find me a pony that week.

Jumping jeepers, was I happy. Living on "cloud nine" was an understatement if it was used to describe me. All I could do was dream of galloping through the fields and pastures, free to go where my will desired. I lived in so much ecstasy, dreaming about my new pony, that, before I realized it, the week was out.

One morning I peered out the window and "glory be," if a truck with a livestock carrier hadn't just driven in the yard. I still find it hard to believe to this day why I wasn't the only excited member of my family. I mean, here was my dream of a lifetime, and the only person in the family that didn't beat me to the truck was my little brother, Jerry!

To my surprise, the man who got out of the truck was none other than Hans Mooseoff, the grumpy old owner of the pony rides at the county fair each year. This fact did little to alter my joy, however. When he got out of his truck, he personally greeted me as though he knew me, and possibly he did remember my annual antics on his ponies at the fair.

"Well, boy, looks like you'll have your own beast to kick now."

I was unsure whether it had been said in sarcasm or plain conversation, but at any rate, I was hoping he would get the lead out so I could see my new pony.

Mr. Mooseoff flung open the door, and, in the back of the truck, stood a sublime, shiny-black, bright-eyed, pony mare. She was already saddled and bridled. Obviously, Dad had thought of everything when he had purchased her.

She was quickly unloaded, and, just as quickly, I was glued in the saddle. The old man, while hanging onto the reins, explained that her name was Lady. Her mother was one of the ponies used in the carnival. He warned me to be cautious for a few days, because she was only a three-year-old pony, just green-broken and extremely frisky.

Before I was allowed to ride off, he asked me if I knew what breed she was. I had to confess that I did not. He then proceeded to explain that she was a Welsh pony. Welsh ponies, unlike their smaller cousins, the Shetland ponies, are powerful and large enough to carry a full-grown man. They are easygoing with children and for this reason are the kinds of pony usually used for carnival rides.

At last it appeared that he had stopped lecturing me. Just as I was about to take off on Lady, he said, "I'll just lead you around for a bit, so you can get acquainted with each other."

What next? I thought to myself.

Finally, he stated, "She's all yours," and off I went. First I walked her to the end of the driveway, then trotted her down the road, and at last turned her into Dad's pasture at a full gallop. The wind was whistling in my ears, and I was laughing so hard I could barely hang on. In just a flash, it seemed we had covered the distance of the pasture, so I turned her around to go back to the house.

It was true that Lady was frisky and full of pep, but, throughout my life, I always preferred the route with more action to it, rather than the opposite. There were times, especially when I first got Lady, when I thought I would be able to audition for a rodeo. Once in a while, if I nudged her in the ribs to go, she gave a couple of bucks, and I actually enjoyed these almost as much as just riding her normally.

On one particular occasion, my mother was entertaining her brother's family with a Sunday dinner and general get-together. My Uncle George also had always had a love for horses, so, before long, George and the rest of the group were outside to see my new pony. I saddled her up and hopped in the saddle as I normally did. This time, though, Lady caught me off guard. In front of my family—aunt, uncle, and all my cousins—she chose to humiliate me royally. I gave her the go-ahead signal, and bang, pow, I was on the hard gravel with a skinned elbow, damaged pride, and an extremely sore behind. I must confess, it was painful, and I believe I may have whimpered slightly. Uncle George, who is a big man, asked my father if this happened often. Dad replied that the young mare did seem to be picking the habit up at an increasing rate.

Well, the next sequence of events was comical, to say the least. George asked if he could ride her, so I said, "Go ahead." It was unreal to see him put his better-than-sixfoot, two-hundred-pound frame on the back of the pony mare. His feet came above the ground by only a couple of inches. I'm sure he had a learning lesson in mind for the mare from the start.

As soon as he was in place on her back, he took her reins in one hand, a handful of her long black mane in the other, and then jabbed her unmercifully in the belly, harder than I ever could. Little Lady let out a disgruntled snort, laid her ears back, and then kicked straight up. When she came down, not only was my large uncle still planted on her back, but he was jabbing her even harder in the belly this time. Lady tried to compensate by twisting around, lowering her head, and bucking again. This went on for a period of time. It seemed everyone was enjoying himself immensely, even George. Lady, however, was another story. She was breathing hard, sweating, and looking as though her bluff had just been called. Suddenly she just peacefully gave up, and, as long as I owned her, she never bucked or acted up again.

When I first acquired Lady, I would ride her down in the pasture all the time. We would go along the creek and see our reflections in the sparkling water. After owning Lady for some time and having gotten adjusted to her, I decided one day to take her across the creek.

I figured the best method would be the all-out run and jump routine. On television, it looked quite easy for the horse to come galloping up to the water and then gracefully bound over, without even missing a step. So Lady and I went back what seemed a fair distance, and then went surging forward. We had a good pace built up, and the creek was approaching fast. Up to the edge we came and then . . . .

Lady had never had direct contact with water, other than drinking it. We always rode next to the water, but she had never so much as set a foot in it. Now I was asking her to fly across. At this point, she decided it was imperative to apply the brakes. As for me, I was anticipating a propelling force in the forward direction, as we were about to jump the creek. I was naturally leaning forward because of this. So here Lady put on the emergency stop, and head over heels I went. This in itself was funny, but one must realize I was too young to swim, and the creek also contained "quick mud," as we always referred to it. It was oozy and grippy. If one stepped in, he could sink in some distance, much as with quicksand. Sure enough, I got stuck right in the mud, to a point near the middle of my thighs.

All that had happened and was about to happen took place quickly. Lady was frightened over the whole matter, so she whirled around to get out of there. My thoughts at that point were not exactly confident either, so I was reaching for anything to pull myself out. Just about then, Lady whirled, her tail flipped around, and, since it was the nearest object to aid in my battle for survival, I latched on. I thought my arms would get yanked from their sockets but, as she took off, the mud let go of me with a loud, sucking noise, and swoosh, through the grass I was pulled. Not wanting to spend much time behind Lady's flying hooves, I released my grip and skidded to a stop.

Everything could have been fine from here on, had it not been for a few minor details. My mother had nearly threatened my life on several occasions for continuously going too close to the swirling waters of the stream. I knew it was dangerous, and Mom based her thinking on sound reasoning, but, then, what young, ambitious boy ever heeded the warning of a paltry spanking when in quest of adventure and exploration? My problem now was that I was living proof of my mother's fears. Only a couple of weeks earlier, Mom had bought me a new pair of farm shoes, and now they were caked, both inside and out, with mud. My clean pants were dripping mud from every stitch. I began desperately devising a plan.

My first chore was to put Lady away without Mom or Dad seeing my external appearance. Luckily, Dad was out in the field somewhere, and Mom was in the house. I quickly tore off the saddle, brushed my pony down, gave her a scoop of oats, and left to carry out step two of my plan.

I took off my abused new shoes and did the best job I could of cleaning them in a watering tank. I was too desperate to debate whether the cattle would appreciate drinking muddy water. I then left my shoes in the sun to dry. Although they were badly stained, I had it figured that Mom or Dad might just not notice how they had lost their shiny, new appearance so rapidly.

Next, I snuck up to behind the old pump house where our trash barrels were kept. I rapidly stripped off my filthy jeans and stuffed them in an old box, inside one of the trash cans. I reasoned that it was better to be minus a pair of pants than face the wrath of one's enraged mother.

Everything was following along according to schedule, when I suddenly realized I had no way to get in the house and put on a pair of pants without my mother seeing me. As I sat there, half-naked and pondering my situation, Mother came out of the door with a basket of clothes to hang on the clothesline. Man, somebody must have been watching out for me that day. She walked with her back toward me, so I padded to the door, opened it quietly, and slid through the opening. I was home free now. I ran to my bedroom, threw on a pair of pants, washed up, and met my mother at the door just as she was coming back in.

"Why, Scott, I thought you went riding this morning. Did you decide not to go?"

"Oh, I did for a while, Mom, but I didn't really have anywhere to ride," I calmly replied.

As I recall the details of that day, I chuckle to myself, because I never did tell my parents about it. They will have to read about it for the first time, along with you.

Four seasons had passed since I first had ridden Lady. Now it was summer again. One day Dad asked me how I would like it if Lady were to have a foal. My answer of yes came before the end of Dad's question. What excited thoughts went through my mind when I envisioned a new baby pony to care for. One day I hoped, I would train him and have as much fun with him as I had had with Lady.

Evidently, Dad had questioned me on a day when Lady was in heat. Only a few hours after my father and I had discussed the matter, Hans Mooseoff, the man we had bought Lady from, drove into the yard with his livestock truck. He jumped out and said to me, "Looks like we'll have to get you a new colt to play with for next year." He walked to the back of his truck and opened the door. Inside was a beautiful, dapple-gray pony stud. His shiny, spotted, gray coat seemed to be pulled so tightly over those bulging rippling muscles. The little stallion's neck was arched, and his nostrils were flared. He had a thick, light-colored mane that flopped around when he moved. We were quickly warned to stand back, because any stallion, be it a pony or a horse, is quite dangerous. They usually have short tempers and will strike out with their legs or try to latch onto you with their teeth. My family heeded the warning and watched Mr. Mooseoff and his pony from a distance.

The next sequence of events still lies in my memory. Lady was in heat, which meant it was the proper time of the month to mate her. Dad led her behind some buildings, and Mr. Mooseoff followed with the little stud, who was, by now beginning to show more than casual interest. Not far behind came Julie, Jerry, and I. All at once, Dad turned around and told Mom to keep us away. Talk about being unfair! Here was my mare, and I couldn't even see what was happening to make her have a colt. I jumped all over Mom, but she just said, "When you kids get a little older, you'll learn about how babies are made."

She did keep her word, because I wasn't much older when my mother sat down to give me my first introduction to the "birds and the bees." That fact, however, was irrelevant, because I was still burned about not being able to go around in back of the building and see the action.

At any rate, they soon came back from behind the building. Dad put Lady back in her pen, and Mr. Mooseoff returned the pony stallion to his spot in the truck. My father paid him some money, and off he drove.

I wanted to act mad, but I was too inquisitive about when the foal would be born, so I quickly forgot about the injustice that had occurred.

Dad explained that a mare must be pregnant for approximately eleven months, and, since it was now June, the baby would be born the following year, during May. For a youngster, that seemed liked an eternity, but, as usual, the time went quickly.

The rest of the summer, I rode Lady as I always had. When winter came, I was sure she got her exercise, but not when the days were too cold. By spring, she was as big as a barrel. I still rode her a little, but not exceptionally hard. My small legs had a hard time straddling her, so I eventually was forced to withdraw from my beloved riding. Soon, May arrived with its green grass, chirping birds, and apple blossoms. My whole family knew the baby foal was just about due.

Lady was put out in a small pasture, which had been fenced off exclusively for her. Each morning Dad would put on his clothes and check on Lady. For two weeks Dad did this but always returned with the same news: nothing. It was almost the end of May. Dad informed me that she could be just a few days overdue, but I still worried. Then on May 31, the last day of May, and also Memorial Day, the foal was born.

My father came running in, yelling, "She had it, she had it." There was a flurry of excitement in our house. In moments we were at the edge of the pasture. There before us was the most darling little fellow we'd ever seen. He had just gotten up on his shaky legs. My sister, Julie, questioned about his name. The whole family, as if it were predestined, agreed that on Memorial Day, his name would have to be Flag.

Flag was the spitting image of his father, with the shiny, dapple-gray coat and light-colored mane. I knew as I watched him stagger toward Lady's back end for his first meal, that my joyous times with him were about to begin.

Flag was all the frisky, frolicking, bundle of energy that one normally associates with a young colt. Strange as it may seem, Flag, like all young foals, was only a fraction the size of his mother, yet he could whisk past her with ease, in one of their early morning romps.

Each day I would spend time with my ponies. Never had I been so happy. Hours would pass as I curried and played with my four-legged friends. Flag grew rapidly, as all young animals do. Before the summer was out, I was teaching him how to lead.

The first instructional lesson involved putting a halter on him. As I slipped the leather contraption over his face, he looked at me with blatant suspicion. Once the halter was secure, I hooked a lead rope up, and off we went, or so I thought. I walked to the end of the rope and then pulled. Flag had other ideas on his mind as he backed up in defiance. There we were, man against beast, in a competitive "tug of war." When finally I thought I could hold my ground no longer, Flag took a great leap. He actually bounded higher in the air distance wise than forward, but at least it was some progress. Evidently, the pulling on his head had begun to hurt, because he soon was taking quick little hops each time I tugged at the rope. At last, after a few rewarding pats and much determination on my part, he was walking along behind me. Flag had come through his first lesson well. As for me, I had many a blister on my hand to show the day's work.

A learning lesson for me came the next summer. I was a 4-H member, and I had kept records on Flag from the time of his birth. The climax for every youngster in 4-H is to show his or her project at the fair. I entered Flag in the halter division of the horse show.

At last, show day arrived. Dad had brought Flag and me to the fair, and, before we knew it, we were lined up in a huge arena. I looked first down one line of horses, then down the other, but I could see no other ponies. I already had enough butterflies in my stomach, so this minor detail did little to upset me further.

Flag had never looked better. I had washed him and then brushed him until his coat just glistened. His mane and tail were long and wavy. He was acting like a pro, so I began to feel better.

I watched as the judge made each contestant walk away from him, then trot his or her animal back toward him. Before long, it was my turn. We proceeded through our exercise in fine form and then positioned ourselves back in the line. When each horse had gone through the motions for the judge, the ribbons were handed out. To my dismay, I received a red ribbon. My pride was hurt, and I wondered what we had done wrong. As all of us left the arena, the judge began to comment on each exhibitor. He stated that my pony had blue-ribbon qualifications, but he had decided to award us with a red ribbon, since I was wearing tennis shoes and not boots. It was later explained to me that, when one works around horses, it's easy to get stepped on. The general feeling is that boots can protect your feet better than tennis shoes. I had learned the hard way, but I did remember my lesson for future occasions.

Time progressed, and I enjoyed my spare moments around the ponies. Whenever I rode Lady, Flag would get jealous, or, if I chose to work with Flag, the jealousy was reversed.

Another year passed, and soon Flag was two years old. This is the magical age when a horse or pony has attained enough skeletal and muscular maturity to support a person on its back. Flag had always been a little feisty, so I knew the breaking process would be a challenge for both of us.

Dad helped by holding Flag. I had already worked for a few weeks on getting Flag used to chomping on a bit and feeling the weight of the saddle on his back. The day arrived when the saddle was to be cinched up and I had to get aboard. As I tightened up the cinch around Flag's belly, he laid his ears back. There was contempt in his eyes, but I still mounted him. I took the reins in one hand, put my feet in the stirrups, grabbed the saddle horn with the other hand, and urged Dad to let him go. Go we did. Up and down, rearing and bucking, sneezing and snorting, we went, until finally Flag was exhausted and my tail bone could no longer take the punishment.

Dad had been laughing so hard, he was almost crying. He said my face was as red as a beet, and apparently I had been trying to hang on so tightly I had forgotten to breathe. In any case, the hard part was over. Oh, Flag still had a few temper tantrums the next few times I rode him, but none was with the "hurricane force" of the first time.

Now with two ponies to ride, I was beside myself with joy.

One day my Uncle Glen asked me if I would like to ride Flag in a parade with him. I assured him I would, so he picked me up, and through the parade we rode that day. I had so much fun riding my little pony next to my uncle's big horse and waving at the crowd that I was disappointed to see the parade end. When the day was over, I was quite sure I would have to try a parade again sometime.

This brings me to a point I alluded to earlier in the book. In the chapter about Tippy, our little fox terrier, I stated that she had some peculiar idiosyncrasies when it came to my ponies and horses.

It all began the first day Lady arrived on the farm. Tippy expressed the usual warm welcome to Lady that she showed to any animal that became a part of the farm. The strange fact was that Lady and Tippy soon became an inseparable pair. Not only would they run and play together, but, from the first time I rode my pony, Tippy took it upon herself to tag along. Quite by accident, I discovered a marvelous trick that Tippy was capable of. I had also mentioned in the earlier chapter about how Tippy had the ability to jump into crotches of trees to scare away birds. Well, one day I got into the saddle for one of my afternoon excursions and said, "Come on, Tippy. Let's go." Then, before I could prod Lady on, Tippy sprang right into my lap. I was extremely surprised, but I decided, as long as she was there, I might as well give her a free ride. Tippy just sat there, smiling and joyously licking my face. After that day, she would often jump up in the saddle with me.

As Lady, Tippy, and I rode around the countryside, we soon became well known by area neighbors and townspeople. What a trio we must have been to spot from one's doorstep!

One summer, our town of Byron had a Centennial celebration. There was to be a big parade, so I entered Lady. The parade day arrived, and, as I left the yard to ride to the parade in town, I told Tippy to stay home for fear she would get hit by a car. Her hurt eyes were more than I could bear, so I told her to hop on, and off we went. That day, we delighted young and old alike as we marched through the streets of Byron. At various points along the parade route, I would give Tippy a little push, and she would jump from the saddle and then spring back up again. All this, mixed with her tail-wagging and smiling usually would evoke quite a round of applause from the onlookers.

I had many more fond memories of my ponies than I could put on paper. This was, however, a sampling of the times I shared with them. Eventually, I outgrew my ponies. By the time I was thirteen years old, they no longer presented an exciting challenge to me. My legs hung beyond their bellies, my little saddle was too small, and neither Flag nor Lady could whisk along at a fast enough paces. I loved my ponies, but inevitably I knew they would have to go. The ponies might have been allowed to stay on the farm, had my younger brother or sister shown any interest in riding. This was an interest they had never developed, though. The law of the farmland is, usually, if there is no more use for something, and it is taking up space as well as feed, then it must go. I realized this and, at last, told Dad that we could try to sell Lady and Flag.

An ad was run in the paper for only a few days, and, before long, my ponies were on their way to new homes. Some fathers and mothers had come to our farm to look at the ponies for their children, much as my father had done a few years earlier for me. I also sold the riding equipment, since I had no further use for it.

I remember talking to both my ponies just before I decided to sell them. I spoke to them as though they understood each word I uttered. It seems odd now to repeat what I said, but at the time it was an exceedingly emotional moment. I stroked both their silky necks, while explaining to them how sorry I was to have to sell them. I told them I loved them and had cherished each moment we'd had together. As you may have guessed, Tippy was right there and she had her tail between her legs as if she knew something sad was happening.

When I walked into the horse trailers with my ponies so they could go to their new homes, I said goodbye to my old friends for the last time. Flag and Lady gently nudged me with their soft noses. As I watched them being driven down the dusty gravel road away from the farm, I knew I would never see them again.

Tippy and I were sad, but inside I was cognizant of the fact that it was only a matter of time before I would start working on Dad to let me have a full-sized horse. For the time being, though, it was necessary for me to get over the loss of my beloved comrades.

5

○ ○ ○ ○

I Won with a Frog

It is my sincere hope that all of the dissertation about frogs in this chapter and the snakes in an earlier chapter does not completely turn everyone's stomach. Perhaps it seems odd that I had such strange pets; however, a brief look back into the annals of history might change one's mind. Surely it isn't difficult to associate Tom Sawyer with frogs, nor other young boys in various different books. I cannot explain why it is when a small boy, such as I was, reaches a certain age—say seven or eight—that a creature such as a frog inevitably becomes a delight to be with. Perchance it has something to do with being at an extremely curious stage of life, or possibly it's just the total grossness of the matter that thrills the pre-adolescent. In any case, I, like many small lads, did not go through my childhood without the mirth of owning a frog and making others squeamish with his presence.

Jerry, my little brother, who was then four years old, was finally at the stage where he and I could do stuff together, and this definitely did not exclude getting into trouble.

It was a fine, sunny, warm spring day on our farm. As usual, the creek running through our pasture was luring me to it like a magnet.

If only our parents could have known exactly how much time we spent at the water's edge, looking for snakes, frogs, and muskrats. On this particular morning we were scouting around near the water for no particular reason, other than, possibly, that Mother didn't want us to. At any rate, Jerry suddenly blurted, "Scott, look at all the funny junk on the water." Sure enough, as I peered over the edge of the bank, there in a little quiet section of the stream was a whole layer of some sort of scum. Without hesitation, we bounded back to the house to inquire of our mother as to its composition.

Mom gave us a quick reprimanding as was normal after we had gone too close to the water and then informed us about our discovery. She said that it could be one of two possibilities: Either it was a thick layer of algae, which is a green plant that grows in the water, or else the frogs around the creek had just laid their eggs. After giving Mom a more detailed description, which told of the little black dots in the substance, she came to the conclusion that it was probably frog eggs.

Boy, were we elated! Almost simultaneously, Jerry and I begged to be able to go back to the creek and get some eggs to hatch out. Luckily, our mother must have at one time or another in her childhood had some contact with frogs and frog eggs, because she wasn't totally opposed to our idea. In fact, she turned out to be of great assistance to us in our endeavor.

Under Mom's supervision and watchful eye, we all went back to the creek carrying some old coffee cans. Jerry and I scooped up some water and then placed a glob of the frog eggs in the cans. They had a sort of cold, clammy, jelly-like consistency to them, but this didn't affect us in any way. The eggs were all kind of attached in large masses. Each little black dot consisted of one egg, and it was surrounded by a clear membrane like jell. There were hundreds of these little black spots and eggs all attached together.

After we had harvested enough eggs for perhaps two hundred frogs, we headed back for the house. On the way back, Mom explained that if we set our cans in the attic where there was no bright light, we would have better luck with the eggs hatching. This we did, and, after closing the door to the attic, we went back outside to find something else to occupy our time.

In the next few weeks the frog eggs were forgotten by Jerry and me, and, unfortunately, by Mom as well. One night, at around eleven o'clock, about three weeks later, while Jerry and I were lying in our bedroom, I suddenly sat up and said with a moan, "Jerry, we forgot about our frog eggs!"

"Oh, oh!" was all he could muster up.

Immediately I fumbled around in the dark for the light, turned it on, and ran to get a flashlight. In a moment I had returned, and we less than bravely headed for the old attic.

Our attic had no lights and seemingly posed little threat during the day time, but somehow at night it just didn't seem like a good place to be.

I opened the door, and naturally it creaked. As I pointed the flashlight into the absolute darkness, I spotted our coffee cans lying in the middle of the floor. I cautiously proceeded forward with Jerry close on my heels. I flashed the light all around, but could see no trace of the hundreds of frogs, which, we had speculated, would be hopping around. Upon reaching the cans, to our dismay, we found that all the water had evaporated. Sometime in the past couple of weeks, the tadpoles, which were the baby frogs, had emerged from their eggs, but, due to our negligence they had shrivelled up and died when the water evaporated.

Jerry and I were quite heartbroken. Now, not only could we not have our frogs to raise, but we had murdered them all besides. To us that was a horrible, double blow to absorb. We carried the cans to the trash containers, put away the flashlight, and then went back to bed for a restless night of sleep.

The next morning, we let the family in on the news, but Mom comforted us immensely. She said that it had only been an accident and went on further to explain that a notably small portion of all the frog eggs that are laid ever become adult frogs. She stated that if it weren't for other animals and the like destroying some of the eggs and tadpoles, the farm would probably be overrun with little green, hopping frogs. This eased our consciences greatly, so, before long, the matter was dropped.

One day not long afterward, I was horsing around by the creek when I noticed the surface didn't have any more eggs on it. Instead, the water was simply infested with little, black, fishlike objects. Yes, these were the newly hatched tadpoles.

The life cycle of a frog goes something like this: First is the egg stage, which has already been discussed. At the proper time for hatching, the little black tadpoles emerge, lacking feet or legs, having only black tails and bodies. In time, providing they escape any predators, their tails will shorten and develop first their back legs, then front legs. To complete the metamorphosis, they completely lose their tails and turn the normal frog color of green and black. At any point, the sight of the tadpoles compelled me to go find Jerry and tell him the good news.

In no time at all, we were sloshing around in the water trying to capture the speedy little future frogs. Each time either of us would catch one, it would be added to the holding pail we had brought with us. At last, we captured about twenty tadpoles and headed for the buildings of our farm to assemble the tadpoles' new dwellings.

After searching for some time, Jerry and I came across an old, fifty-gallon barrel that Dad had cut in half at one time and used as a watering tank for some of his calves. It appeared to fit our idea of a frog home, so we set out to prepare it. We placed the barrel by Dad's big cement silo, because it was a protected spot, then added some water to it. Finally we placed a bunch of rocks on one side, so, when the tadpoles grew their legs, they could get out of the water if they desired to. The tadpoles were then added to their new home, and we spent the next few weeks delightedly catching flies for their meals and watching them slowly change from fishlike forms into young frogs. I must say that this was extremely educational for my brother and me. No doubt, however, if our mother or teachers had mentioned in the beginning that it was a good learning experience, we probably wouldn't have touched it for anything.

In only a matter of weeks, our tadpoles had become transformed into adult frogs. It appeared that now was the chance to utilize their possible resources. In the city of Rochester lived my mom's twin sister, Mary; her husband, Glen; and their children, Diane, Sharon, Chuck, and Bonnie. Since these cousins were children approximately the same age as the children in my family, we spent many joyous occasions together. It so happened that on a particular upcoming Saturday, their elementary school was having a pet parade, and prizes were going to be awarded to the top pets. My cousins had received permission from their teachers to invite our family, and the invitation was happily accepted. Neither my brother, Jerry, nor my sister, Julie, wanted to participate in the event, but I decided to accept the challenge. After all, on a farm such as we had, one might think some sort of animal could be chosen to represent the family. It didn't take me long to decide that a frog in a pet parade of mostly city children would certainly not be considered customary or conventional and might just possibly be a winning entry.

Saturday arrived, and it was totally unnecessary to prepare my frog in any way for his big debut. Well, really, how can one wash and brush a frog? One certainly can't tie a ribbon in his fur or clip his toenails. My biggest decision, though, came in trying to decide which of my twenty frogs to choose. After all, they were not all similar. Some were fat, and some were thin. There were frogs who would hop at a touch and others that would sit and hold their ground.

In looking over the situation, I decided that a big, fat frog with a lot of hopping action would be the most captivating to the judges of the parade. I placed my chosen amphibian in a container and sped to the house where my mother was waiting in the already-running car with Julie and Jerry to take us to the city.

As we jumped out of the car at the school, we were met by our cousins. They had brought along their dog for the parade. In looking about, I was not surprised to see a large assortment of both cats and dogs, but little else. One young girl had a furry rabbit, but I definitely saw no other frogs. My cousins thought it was neat that I had brought my frog, and, just as they were peering into his container for a closer look, the officials announced that the parade would start.

Now the parade consisted of little more than a mere walk around the playground in front of the spectators, who were either parents or children who had not entered any pets. Just before going into the parade lineup, though, I added my last little innovation. Out of my pocket I pulled a piece of string and then proceeded to tie it around the frog's neck in the form of a collar and leash. The added effect worked wonders. As the miniature parade made it rounds, much attention was drawn to the frog in my left hand and the leash I held him with in my right hand. It was as I had felt back on the farm, while deciding on my pet. The children in the city had lots of opportunities to see cats and dogs, but what a thrill it was for them to see a real live frog in the flesh.

I imagine that originality and crowd approval had some weight in the judges' decisions on the winner, but the end result was that my frog and I were victorious and received a small trophy as a reminder of that day.

I still chuckle some when I remember my cousins uttering in dismay after the contest how well they might have done if they had only thought to bring their pet turtle.

Mom was going to allow us all to go over to our cousins to play for a while, but, in the rush to get to the parade, I had completely forgotten to bring any water for my frog. The fact that a frog is an amphibian does allow it to be away from water, but the day was particularly warm and my frog's skin looked dry. The frog began to appear rather woozy, so I urged Mom to get me home quickly. One may ask why I did not get water for the frog at my cousins' house. This I had considered, but the city water had chlorine in it, which is harmful to water creatures. It was therefore decided the get-together with our cousins would have to wait for another day.

After Mom rushed us back to the farm again, I sprang out of the car and put the frog back in the barrel with all his buddies. In no time at all, he was back to normal.

Not long after the pet parade, there was an odd occurrence. I had spent some time as usual searching for flies to feed my frogs. When I felt I had gathered enough, I went to the frog abode, and, much to my surprise, I could find only seventeen of the original twenty frogs. I fished around in the barrel of water, looked under the rocks, and gazed all around the vicinity, but I could locate none of the absent frogs. Unable to understand, I simply fed the remaining ones and went about my daily duties.

The next day I went through the same process, and this time, as I came to the barrel with a quota of flies, I could only find ten frogs. About this time, however, it began to dawn on me that perhaps the little green devils were jumping out of their haunt. Even as I stood there surveying the situation, one frog jumped out. It amazed me how the powerful-legged frog was able to clear the fairly steep sides of the barrel with such ease. I didn't hesitate to quickly replace him, but, as though he knew he had the capability of escaping again, out he vaulted. Then, to my astonishment, the frog chose a direct, hopping path toward the creek, which was several hundred yards away in the pasture. It was at this point that I made the decision to gather him, as well as the other frogs, and return them to their native waters.

When my task was completed, I somehow felt a relief at knowing my group of green friends was back where it belonged. In analyzing my experiences with the frogs, I began to understand why these events had taken place. It all broke down to the fact that my frogs had grown large enough and strong enough and had attained enough of an instinctive desire for the nearby water, which was not far away, that they soon began a massive escape. Evidently, the first few frogs to evacuate had begun the trek toward the stream and most likely had made it safely. Now at least, with my aid, they were all back in their places of birth.

I cannot venture to say whether or not in the future I will ever take up my permanent residence next to a frog-inhabited stream. If so, I hope my children are able to engage in the same unintended learning experiences and memorable times that I had.

6

○ ○ ○ ○

Chickens and
Eggs, Eggs, Eggs

Oddly, it doesn't seem like so many years ago, when my father elected to make a stab at a poultry egg operation. Odd, though, because it is quite a few years in the remote past, but the stress of that endeavor still survives in the minds of my family.

My father had grown up on a dairy farm, and because of his love for it, he had obviously chosen dairying for his present farm. Sadly, however, because of the conflicts with a job he carried on the side, the beloved dairy business was terminated after only a couple of years. Determined to make a go of their farm, my father and mother tenaciously chose a poultry operation as an alternative. It was revealed to the family that, because of the nature of a laying operation, Jerry, Julie and I, at the ages of four, six, and eight respectively, would be able to apply our labor to the enterprise, thus giving Dad more time for both the farm and his job. Being young as we were, we neither had much say in the matter, nor did we know what we were being led into, but before long, there was to be many an egg-laying chicken on the property.

Mom and Dad had done copious research and checked with many a so-called "authority" about adapting the farm for poultry. When they were satisfied with the "facts and figures," they began implementing their burdensome task.

Before the new endeavor could be started, the dairy operation was auctioned off. I watched my father sadly see his dairy cows disbursed to various parts of the country. It was just as it had been only a few short years earlier, when he had sold our first farm. It's difficult to understand what must go through a person's mind when he observes something he's loved and strived for suddenly vanish without his having much choice in the matter. Yes, my stalwart father always did a good job holding his emotions within, but I know that, deep down, he struggled with many sentiments.

When the last cow, last milk pail, and last dairy relic of any kind had left the farm, we set to work on the next priority. That priority was housing for the chickens. There were to be three chicken buildings, none of which had originally been built for the purpose of an egg-laying operation. For sake of ease, my Father assigned an "A," "B," and "C" lettering system on the buildings. The A building was none other than our old dairy barn and hayloft. Within only a week, its insides had been sawed, nailed, and redistributed into what at least appeared to be a chicken-house. Ventilation fans were put into the walls, and feeders, waterers, and egg-laying nests were put in not only the bottom of the barn where the cows had been, but also up in the hayloft. The barn was to be a loose housing system where the chickens were allowed to be free in the building. This was not to be the case in buildings B and C.

Building B had been a large, round-roofed, tin quonset machine shed where the farm's tractors and equipment were kept. Again, however, within a couple of weeks, it was no longer a machine shed.

This time a ceiling, walls, insulation, lights, and ventilation fans were all added. In addition to these, a meticulous, systematic-looking, caged-hen laying system was put in the renovated building. Several rows of cages that were layered three high, soon lined the building. Each cage was to hold five hens, although it appeared that one chicken would have had a tight squeeze. The chickens were watered and fed in the cages with automatic feeders and waterers. To further cut down on the labor, when an egg was laid by a hen, it gently rolled down the slanted floor of the cage to the front, for easy access during egg collection.

Finally the remodeling of building C was underway. The execution now seems even more absurd than it had for the first two buildings. My father determined that constructing a new chicken house would be much too expensive. It was because of this that he found a somewhat decently structured hog house to use as building C. Dad found a farmer who had a good-condition, approximately sixty-foot-long hog barn that was no longer in use. My father paid him a fair price, and then hired some hauling men to move the complete building several miles to our farm. Once it was there, water pipes, electricity, fans, and the cages were all added. When complete, it had the same lines of cages as buildings B, but these cages were only layered two high instead of three. In any case, to this day, I think Dad would have been better off building a chicken house from scratch, rather than going through all the turmoil of updating the old building. I, for sure though, would never tell him that.

The day arrived when the young pullets were to be introduced on to the farm. All the feeders were full, the waterers, were turned on, the fans were purring, and the empty buildings almost appeared as though they were anticipating the new arrivals.

Just after dinner on that sunny Saturday afternoon, several trucks drove in. The trucks carried literally thousands of young female chickens. The rest of the day my whole family and the several truckers distributed close to six thousand birds in the three different laying houses. By nightfall, buildings A, B, and C were no longer filled with a subtle stillness, but now seemed to fairly buzz with avian noises and the flapping of wings.

If we had only known what we were getting into. I must have repeated that phrase a million times to Jerry and Julie. It appeared that our gleeful childhood days had been suddenly plucked from us. Now each day was filled with hours of monotonous chores, chores that left little time to play or have fun. Many a day went by when my siblings and I were too "dog tired" to play anywhere. Oh, sure, in the beginning it wasn't bad. The young pullets were too immature to be in the laying stage, and all the feeding was done by Dad, who, with boyish enthusiasm would trust no one but himself. The problem, however, arose when the eggs began to come. It was slow at first. Ten eggs one day, fifty in a day or two, then two hundred, and before long three or four thousand eggs a day were being collected!

It was Dad's choice to be on a grade-double-A, certified egg program. This was where the most money was, but rigid standards of egg quality had to be met on a monthly basis. It was also Mom and Dad's decision to sell all of our eggs "private treaty." This way we could reap all the profits, instead of having a big slice taken out to have a produce man buy the eggs and distribute them.

The whole process involved when selling one's own eggs is quite complicated, but my father was more than determined to accomplish that goal. He first went out and bought himself a van, then had it painted up professionally with our name and phone number on it. Next he, more or less, went door to door and solicited customers for our eggs. I can hardly believe now, as I reminisce back to those days, how many customers we handled. Some of them included three area schools, major grocery-store chains, restaurants, and dairy produce stores from three cities, including the city of Rochester. When, finally, enough outlets for our eggs had been attained, my father spent several hours each day delivering the eggs, while Mom and we children stayed home to slave away. One can hardly realize what must go on behind the scenes in an operation of this dimension.

The eggs were collected in rubber-coated, wire egg baskets three times a day. All egg-gathering was done by Jerry, Julie, and me, except for the midday collection while we were in school, and that was done solely by Mom. I must admit that this farming operation was truly a family effort. Each of us three children would grab a basket. Jerry, being the youngest, would take the bottom row of cages; Julie, the middle; and I, being the oldest, would take the top.

We did have our problems, though. For one, I was only eight and not exactly tall for my age, so, in order to reach the top layer of the cages and gather the eggs, it was necessary for me to get on my very tiptoes. Not only was this extremely uncomfortable after a couple of hours, but, even when I stretched out, I could barely get over the wire lip at the end of the cage to get the eggs. The result was that each day I would have a sorely bruised and sometimes scratched wrist. In time, however, I outgrew the problem.

Jerry and Julie also had their problems. Each basket, when full, held approximately one hundred eggs. My brother and sister, being only four and six years old, had a rough time getting around with those heavy baskets. They also eventually outgrew their problems.

To this moment, I must laugh when I think of it, because my brother Jerry still is almost bitter about what he had to do at that tender age. We had a type of pecking order among the children, whereby the most unappealing jobs were distributed down the line according to age. When gathering eggs in the loose-housing system, Julie and I would pick eggs from the nest. Poor Jerry would have to crawl around on the floor and underneath the nests with all the manure and gather eggs from chickens that wouldn't lay in the nests.

Another job Jerry was stuck with was disposing of the dead chickens. Beyond the farm building was a large pit that was completely sealed, except for a small door that could be opened. It was in this pit that all the dead birds were tossed. Here bacteria speeded up the decomposition of the dead chickens in a process similar to that of a septic tank. Gratefully, this was accomplished with little odor being produced. The job was quite distasteful, because, with several thousand chickens all cramped in tight spots, it was not uncommon and totally acceptable to lose between ten and thirty a day. The other members of the family helped Jerry as often as they could, but, for the most part, he was the sole mortician for the deceased birds. Most of his agony came when a chicken that had been dead for several days was detected at last by its odor. Sometimes it would be so rotten by this time that the feathers would be denuded, maggots would be embedded in the flesh, and pieces of the chicken would easily pull off. I don't mind saying I felt sorry for my little brother at times such as these when he would have to carry those foul-smelling birds to the pit in one hand, and hold his nose with the other hand. Thank goodness, at least, now, we can look back on times such as those and laugh.

Although it seemed an unfair burden to put on such a little fellow as my brother, it was necessary, because everyone was carrying more than an adequate share of the workload. What had to be done from the time the chicken laid the egg, until it was bought in the store or eaten in a restaurant was a time-consuming and joyless job. Once the eggs were gathered, they were brought to the egg house and washed with an automatic egg washer. They were next put in egg flats, but the eggs that hadn't been adequately cleaned were hand cleaned first.

Once in the flats, the eggs were transferred immediately to the large, walk-in egg cooler. Then, each day's supply of eggs was taken and processed by the whole family. I would take the eggs from the flats and transfer them to the automatic egg candler and scale. Mom would stand and view the two columns of eggs as they passed over the bright lights in the machine and check for bloodspots, cracks, or any other abnormalities in the eggs. The machine would then take those columns of eggs, weigh them out and deposit them in various holding areas for extra-large, large, medium, or small eggs. It was at this station that Dad stood, and he could quickly fill up a carton of eggs with two swift motions by taking three eggs in each hand and quickly, but gently, putting them in the cartons. At another table not far away, Jerry and Julie would take the boxed eggs from Dad, add the appropriate grade-AA labels, and then box the cartons in cases for Dad's deliveries. This whole process was repeated each day for about four years, and, believe me, it was torture.

I remember riding with Dad on occasion with several hundred cartons of eggs in the back of the van on our way to make deliveries. I used to enjoy running up to the loading dock and ringing the bell in the backs of the stores so they would open up. Usually while I was doing this, Dad was backing his van up to the door. As I helped him unload the proper quantities at each place, I always felt like such a big shot. On one particular trip, however, it was snowing out, and the road was quite slippery. I was sitting in the front seat with Dad, and Jerry was sitting in the back with the egg cases. We were just about to turn off the road and make a turn, but, as Dad put on the brakes, the van began to skid. Right head-on, into a sign, we plummeted, and all the cartons of eggs came crashing forward upon Jerry, Dad, and me. The van sustained only a little dent in the bumper, but almost two hundred and fifty cartons of eggs were "scrambled," one might say. I suppose that was the price to be paid for working with such a fragile commodity.

One other outlet for our eggs was developed by my parents. The area farmers and townspeople always wanted to buy eggs, so my father and mother devised an "on-your-honor" buying system. They put a portable egg cooler, a shelf, cashbox, and the various egg prices in our garage. People could come any time of the day or night, carton their eggs, and pay for them. It was a marvelous system that saved a lot of time, and in the two years of use, it was only abused by dishonest customers two or three times.

Another dreadful segment of the chicken operation came around about once a month when it was time to clean out the chicken buildings. Since I was the oldest child, and Dad didn't want Mom to do that kind of work, I was chosen to help him. The rigorous job consisted of scooping the heavy, malodorous poultry waste from under the cages, putting it in a wheelbarrow, wheeling it out to the manure spreader, and then shoveling the contents into the spreader. It was a job that took several days at the end of each month, but it did build strong bodies and appetites, of that I am sure.

Chickens are extremely touchy creatures. Because they are a production type of animal, care must be taken not to upset them or their schedules in any way. I distinctly remember one miserable winter, the winter of 1967, when a blizzard hit Minnesota with overwhelming fury. We had evergreen trees in our yard that were twenty to twenty-five feet high, and Jerry, Julie, and I were walking up the drifts and over the treetops. This particular blizzard hit with such force that it knocked out power lines for a couple of days. That was where our trouble began.

The road from our house was so snowed in, it had to be plowed with a caterpillar days later. The chicken facilities were a disaster. We couldn't feed or water them with the automatic system, so we hand fed them. Because the water pump was out, we had to take water from the cattle tanks for the chickens, and let the beef cows eat snow. The buildings had no lights or ventilation, and the insides just reeked of ammonia. Even our house had no heat, water, or electricity. For two days we sat, shivered, and wondered when the power would be restored. At last, the lights came on, but more problems were still in store.

For several days after the incident, not just Jerry, but all my family members were hauling as many as three hundred dead hens a day to the pit. For weeks after the power failure, the hens laid remarkably few eggs; in fact, that particular batch of hens was never normal again and most definitely proved to be a losing undertaking.

The times with the poultry setup were not all bad. I took some chickens to the fair for 4-H and FFA projects and won blue ribbons with them. Also the knowledge I gained in working with poultry led me to become one of the top poultry judges in FFA.

There were some personal experiences with certain chickens that seem quite idiotic now, but not so much then. One of the hens, whose abode was a certain cage in building B, would cackle in the exact manner of a classmate of mine in school. His name was Joe, and soon the whole family began calling this audible hen, "Joe, the Laugher."

Another hen found a soft spot in the hearts of my brother and me. She was a big, fat hen that apparently was at the bottom of the hen-pecking order and was picked on by all the other hens in the loose-housing system of building A. The other chickens had pecked at her head on several occasions, until all her feathers were gone and her scalp was a mass of scabs and scars. Feeling sorry for her, Jerry and I would pet her and protect her from attackers whenever we were in the building. She became known to us as "Scarhead," and, when we found a hen picking on her, we would retaliate in her behalf. Chickens are not only cannibalistic at times, but also love to fight. What we would do to any Scarhead tormentor was to capture her, set her on the ground, grab her feet, and rustle her back and forth. To the other hens, this was an outright sign of a challenge, and the tormentor was soon the tormented, as a flock of twenty hens attacked it. Because the other hens would not let Scarhead in the nests, she could always be found laying an egg in one of the feeders. When Jerry and I gathered eggs each day, the feeders were the first places we checked. To our horrible dismay, we found Scar-head dead one day. Ironically, she had died while trying to lay a double-yolked egg, which is a double-sized egg that happens on occasion by mistake. Evidently, the stress had been too much. I wouldn't say we had a funeral for her, but we did miss the old, friendly hen for some time after that.

"Boys will be boys" was exactly what could be said for my brother and me, with some of the pranks we enjoyed together. Jerry and I would occasionally get in a spunky mood while gathering eggs. It would start with one of us throwing an egg at the other, and, before long, we would be bombing away like crazy. Each of us would hide in a corner of the chicken house and zing dozens of eggs back and forth. One might say it was a modified snowball fight. In any event, there were never any telltale signs, because the hens would lap up the broken eggs, shell and all without a trace. Dad never caught us, because, due to the sensitive nature of laying hens, it was always just assumed the egg output was down a bit for the day. Jerry and I never told Dad or Mom about this, and in a way it brings a little guilt into my mind when I think of the money we were actually throwing away, simply because of plain immaturity. I have a sneaking suspicion, however, that when my father does read this, he'll still "tan our hides," even though it's been years and years since chickens have been a part of the farm.

In a nutshell, there were some good times and some bad times in relation to the poultry setup. For instance, Jerry and I received nicknames from our peers at school, such as "Chickenman" and "Superchicken" and there could be no mistaking the fact that we were unmatched at making chicken calls, but the stress the operation brought our parents was immeasurable. We were in poultry at a time when it just wasn't a very profitable business. Now, with operations consisting of tens of thousands of birds, and complete push-button systems from manure-handling to egg collection, as well as better egg prices, the laying operations appear to be doing better. My parents were in their operation when prices were bad, and it just took too much time, money, and labor to get the necessary production. Unknown to us children, my parents fought a struggling financial battle for many years. At the end of each year, the laying hens had eaten away thousands of dollars more in feed than they had produced in eggs. My poor mother bore the last two members of our family while under a terrible strain. Sally was born only hours after my mother had finished her complete set of heavy and strenuous chores, which she had continued, throughout her pregnancy, without letup. Marcia was born a couple of years later under similar circumstances.

Mom and Dad had undertaken a losing proposition from the start and were determined to make it good. The problem was, it just never went anywhere. At last, Dad decided enough was enough. He weaned off all his customers and sold the thousands of chickens to a soup company for a paltry three cents a pound. At last, the nightmare was over, but the bills and debts were still to be paid.

As I look back on those trying times, I often wonder how we struggled through. I guess the point is, we did make it with the love of God and a powerful family bond that will forever exist.

The farm went into other more profitable operations soon afterward, and all that was left of the experience was just the shadow of a memory.

7

○ ○ ○ ○

A Nightmare with Rats

"Jerry! Jerry! One is in my bed!"

"Oh Scott! What are we going to do? They're all over the room!"

Imagine if you will the impact an activity must need to have on two people to create the same frightening dream. Jerry and I were having nightmares about rats, of all creatures, and—believe me—the dreams were terrifying.

In the previous chapter I outlined the whole process that was involved in our poultry and egg-laying operation. I explained how my family broke into the business, how we strived to make it successful, and, finally, how we exited from the financial burden of that endeavor. Yes, all the chickens were removed from the premises, and, as one might expect, my father and I were left with the monstrous task of cleaning the manure from all of the buildings. Neither of us really balked on this occasion, though, because, thankfully, it was to be the last time. Within a span of two weeks, the once-full hen buildings were finally empty and clean. Unknown to anyone in my family, however, a new problem was about to surface.

I had previously made mention of rats and explained that all farms are cursed with these rodents, no matter how neat and well kept up the farmstead might have been. These slinky, long-tailed, creatures except possibly for their albino cousins in the scientific research world, are of little benefit to mankind. The common gray rat, throughout history, has been a sign of famine, disease, and unsanitary conditions. On the farm, these animals take up residence in walls, under buildings, in hay, or anywhere else that can provide them with shelter, food, and a place to proliferate. It was no secret to my family that, soon after we began the poultry operation, many rats moved in. This is often the case in enterprises such as ours, in which there is an abundance of spilled feed for the rats to consume. Evidently, an easy point of entry for them was through cracks in the foundations of our various buildings. I have no idea how rats communicate, but it always appeared to me that when a new place for them to exist was constructed, word traveled quickly. They must have moved into the new dwellings by the hordes during the night, but, oddly and quite characteristically, hardly one was ever detected.

Once the rats had established themselves in the chicken houses, it was virtually impossible to eradicate them, even though we tried every way imaginable.

When we were first starting in poultry, the rat problem was small and almost undetectable, but, within months, it had mushroomed. Rats can breed at an unbelievable rate, and, by having almost unlimited food supplies, that's exactly what they did. Before long, the buildings my father had fixed up for the chickens were riddled with large rat-holes. The rodents were nothing more than large parasites that were robbing the laying operation of feed and money. Dad decided something had to be done.

Poison was our first strategy. We placed container after container of poison by each rat hole in the buildings. For a few days it was eaten, but, as though the rats knew it was dangerous, the poison suddenly stopped being consumed. This, however, was not much of a surprise to my dad. He had somehow suspected that the poison would not be eaten, especially with such an unlimited supply of fresh poultry feed available. In his determination to win the battle, he turned to other tactics.

One day Dad came home with a whole bag full of rat traps. They were huge steel contraptions, and I was sure this would produce some positive results. Each trap was baited with a little dab of peanut butter, the powerful spring snap was pulled back, and finally all the traps were set ominously in front of the many holes. As was expected, nothing happened that day, since rats are mainly nocturnal beasts, but we were quite surprised the next morning. Dad and I came charging into one of the henhouses expecting to see dozens of trapped rats, but, to our amazement, out of all the traps that had been laid, only one small, young rat had been captured. Incredulously, disbelievingly, my father and I looked at each other and secretly asked ourselves just what type of foe we were up against. Each day from then on we checked the traps, but the result was constantly negative. In the several weeks the traps lay waiting, only half a dozen small, young rats, at the most, were ever captured. Never was an adult rat lured into the jaws of the traps.

At last my father gave up the battle. It appeared that, whatever measure was taken against the rats, the victory was always theirs. I often wondered as to the true magnitude of our farm's rat population. It has often been agreed that for every rat that is spotted or caught, there are one hundred more in the population that no one ever sees. If this information is true, then we were supporting probably in excess of a thousand rats.

This brings me to the events that led Jerry and I to our nightmares. As I mentioned earlier, my parents disbanded the poultry operation. Several days later, with the hens gone, the manure cleaned out, and no feed left, a new problem was developing. The swarms of rats that were in the attics and walls of the now empty buildings were starving. Eventually they would have moved on to more optimal areas, but my conscientious father and mother decided not to pawn our gray enemies off on the neighboring farms.

Dad went out and brought back gallons of rat poison. He placed adequate amounts in each building, along with plenty of fresh water for the rats to drink. The active ingredient in rat poison is an anticoagulant, which literally caused the rodents to hemorrhage to death internally. At first the rats were finicky about eating, but hunger soon lured them out. Before long, Jerry and I were spending a portion of each day disposing of dead rats in the pit that we had previously thrown dead chickens into. Dad took particular care in making sure that our farm cats and dogs had no contact with the rats, particularly since they in turn could become poisoned if they consumed one of the dead rats.

In the first few days of the poisoning, Jerry and I would go into the spooky, old, empty chicken houses at night to "hunt rats" as we called it. To this day, I am unsure of why we did this. My whole family, like other people, had a phobia when it came to rats, and we were defying all our basic instincts in playing this game. I, manned with a large crowbar, and Jerry, holding a flashlight, would fling open the door of one of the buildings, flip on the lights, and watch as up to fifteen hungry rats went scampering for their holes. We would then proceed to go in, close the door, shut off the lights in the windowless building, and station ourselves by a heavily used rat hole. We would sit and literally shake in the dark as we listened to the noises and squeaking of several rats running about in the walls and across the ceiling up in the attic. After a few moments in the intimidating dark, Jerry would flick on his flashlight and point it at the hole. Many times a blinded and dazed rat would be at the entrance of the hole, or sometimes one would simply be passing by the opening.

I would then take my trusty crowbar and thrust it into the hole after the rat. On many an occasion I would connect, and the battle would begin. For instance, one time, a huge male rat came wandering past the hole, and I jabbed the cold, steel crowbar into his side. I thought "all hell" would break loose after that. The rat, which seemed as large as a dog, started screeching at the top of his lungs. Jerry and I immediately imagined the same dreadful thought of how this possible leader of the rodent colony was calling for assistance. All I could think of was that at any moment several rats would come leaping through the air to attack us.

"Jerry, hurry up and hit the lights," I screamed.

Quickly my brother threw on the switch, and for the moment we were at least relieved to be out of the darkness of doom. Unfortunately, my present situation left much to be desired. I twisted and turned my weapon, trying to destroy the rat, but he wouldn't give in.

With the sweat pouring from my brow and the angry rat maliciously screaming at me, I blurted, "Quick, Jerry—go get Dad to help us."

Jerry turned and ran, but, before he had cleared the door, I again cried, "Wait! Don't leave me in this place alone."

"What are we going to do, Scott?" Jerry frantically returned.

"Well, you stand at the door and start shouting. Dad or Mom is bound to hear you."

Sure enough, Dad had heard Jerry's distraught cries, and in moments he was running through the door gasping for breath and demanding to know what was wrong. Without waiting for an answer, he sized up the dilemma, pulled out a hammer and began assisting me. He swung several times at the rat I had pinned, and at last the disgusting creature lay still with what one might classify as a severe, "splitting" headache.

Dad tried to pull the large, male rat from the hole, but he couldn't squeeze him through. After he had enlarged the hole somewhat, the rat fell to the floor. The size of that fellow was incredible. The dead rats that Jerry and I had been throwing in the pit were only about half the size of this monster. I realized at that point that it had been no fluke when I had difficulty in putting an end to him. At any rate, Jerry and I were relieved that the ordeal was over.

Dad mildly scolded us for playing this possibly dangerous game and warned against further pranks. We assured him, however, that a second warning would not be necessary.

That same night, Jerry and I went to bed in the room we shared together. The whole night was one protracted nightmare. We had finally reached our saturation point in dealing with rats, and they were weighing heavily on our minds.

First, I would cry, "Jerry, watch out! There's another one!"

Then my brother would shout, "One's on my leg, Scott! Help! Get Dad!"

I can remember vividly lying in my bed with a cold sweat covering my body. I had completely tucked all the covers on my bed tightly around my body and over my head. By morning, Jerry and I woke up and our pajamas were soaked with perspiration. To our surprise, we had dreamed the exact same dreams, done the same actions through the night, and had actually conversed in our frightened, demented sleep.

We were both quite comforted to see the sunrise. Later that morning, we were able to laugh about the whole affair.

As the days passed, fewer and fewer dead rats were recovered. In a couple of weeks the poison was no longer being eaten. The time had finally come when the old chicken houses were totally empty and silent at last.

Thankfully, Jerry and I were only to experience that horrifying nightmare once in our lifetimes. We still, on occasion, think back and reminisce about that day. For us, though, this was an encounter with the animal kingdom that we didn't care to repeat.

8

○ ○ ○ ○

A Different Sort of Dog

Our boxer dog was built to a tee like any bulldog ever depicted on a television cartoon. He had a massive, muscular head with slobbery, droopy lips. His head was connected to a behemoth set of shoulders, which quickly tapered into what seemed a small rear end for such a large dog. His odd-looking features were topped off with a tiny, stubbed tail, which sped back and forth with amazing swiftness on any happy occasion.

We acquired him in a strange sort of way. My mother was a secretary for our school in Byron. One day she came home and told of a predicament her boss, the school superintendent, was in. Apparently, his family had bought a puppy whose dam had been a purebred, registered boxer and whose sire had been a German shepherd. Evidently, this family had known little about dog sizes or habits, because they were desperately looking for a new home to suit their rapidly growing pup. Mom told of how her boss had said he had had no idea how large the dog would get. His family had originally bought him for a house pet, but the king-sized messes he accidentally made, along with an ability to tear up any part of the house he desired, had made them decide to part with him.

Naturally my brother, sister, and I listened intently to the story and then begged to have him, as any group of young children would. I don't really think we could have lost in this instance, because Mom was for it to start with.

At first Dad held his ground, saying, "We don't need another dog around here. Tippy is just fine."

Poor Dad was so outnumbered, though; he gave in after only a short time. We were instructed to get into the car, and we gladly piled in so we could go and pick up our new dog.

When we were all in the superintendent's house, the giant of a puppy came smashing around a hallway corner to greet us. Everyone immediately began laughing at his huge paws, flopping lips, and racing little tail. Mom's boss said he was so glad we were going to give Pepper a good home.

Immediately I looked at Julie and whispered, "Pepper! What kind of a name is that?"

Mom's boss continued to talk and told of how it was strange that the puppy looked so much like a boxer, even with a German shepherd sire. As we observed, it was true that the pup was brown, white chested, black muzzled, and had the characteristic offset, under biting jaws of a full-blooded boxer.

My Dad said, "It looks to me like the only traits he got from his sire were his slightly longer snout and large size."

With that, the family and puppy piled into the car and headed for home. I assure you, however, before we reached the farm's driveway, the family had happily agreed to rename Pepper with a more fitting name—Muggs.

Tippy, our little fox terrier, and Muggs hit it off well from the start. It was almost as though Tippy was glad to have a playmate to spend the day with. Muggs was obviously ecstatic over the wide open spaces he saw, especially after being cooped up in that little house.

Muggs, like any other animal, had a unique personality, which didn't take long to surface. Soon after we acquired him, Muggs started a lifelong habit. What was the habit, one might ask? Sleeping. Yes, Muggs had some of the effervescence of a young puppy, but, for the most part, he enjoyed plunking down in the nice warm sun and snoozing for hours on end. My family always maintained that the phrase "a dog's life" had surely been made for Muggs. The funniest part, though, was when Muggs would awake from a deep slumber. He would crack everyone up, because, when he opened his eyes, one could see that they were depressed way down in their sockets. Then, like two balloons, they would float to their normal positions. His eyes were always red rimmed after he woke up, and it took several minutes to get them back to their normal, white color. As soon as Muggs was awake, he would always get up, yawn deeply and loudly, then stretch by putting both front paws out in front of his body. It was no exaggeration, then, to say that sleeping was exactly how Muggs spent 75 percent of his life.

About the time Muggs became a member of our farm family, I was looking for a new 4-H project. It so happened there was a dog project, and the great part was that, in the city of Rochester, a lady was giving dog obedience classes to young 4-H kids. A dog show was to be put on at the county fair at the end of the training, as the final reward for our hard work.

Mom and Dad were almost as excited as I was. Our family had never had a finely trained dog that would do various tasks on command. This, perhaps, was the chance to own such a dog. The day arrived for the first class, and the whole family piled into the car for the occasion. Earlier I had spent almost an hour brushing Muggs so he would look respectable. I had put on his new training collar and fastened the leather leash that Mom had bought. At last, the moment had arrived to take Muggs to his training session, so into the car we went and off to the first class.

Not far down the road, we learned something new about Muggs: he got carsick. He had been sitting on the floor, looking rather uncomfortable, and all of a sudden he just sat up, put his head on Julie's lap and vomited all over her. Needless to say, she lost all respect for Muggs. After that day we always transported Muggs in the back of the pickup truck.

After getting Julie and the car cleaned up, we were ready for the first obedience class. The woman who was our instructor had brought her dog to give us a demonstration. He was a fine-looking German shepherd and without a leash did all sorts of tricks and maneuvers on her command. The dog would sit, heel, lie down, "come," and jump, simply on her word alone. The crowd of people was quite impressed, and no one could wait until his own dog would be able to perform in such a fashion. At last we were asked to bring our pets forward. There were approximately thirty dogs present, representing almost every breed, size, and shape. Muggs was the only boxer and by far the youngest of the dogs. The lady told me that Muggs might be too young to learn everything, but the class would surely do him good.

From that day on, Muggs and I worked constantly on his obedience. The class met once a week for several weeks, and each spare moment of the day was spent in practice. Muggs seemed to have a real knack for his training, because he always performed up to my highest expectations. By the end of the obedience classes, Muggs could do several obedience maneuvers without a flaw. The instructor was always impressed at how well he behaved by never barking or disrupting the class as several other dogs often did. At the last class before the fair, the instructor did a test procedure to see how our dogs could cope with the noise of the fair. We had our dogs lie down and commanded them to stay. We then walked to the other end of the room. The instructor took a large coffee can and tossed it down the line of dogs, right in front of their noses. All but two dogs jumped quickly to their feet and ran in fright. One of the dogs still lying down was Muggs, and he was staring blankly into space, most likely trying to ward off sleep. After that, I was sure Muggs and I had a blue ribbon all wrapped up for the next week's fair.

At the fair my hopes of a blue ribbon were shattered. Even though Muggs had performed magnificently until now, his young age and immaturity really surfaced the day of the dog show. He was so distracted by all the commotion that he wouldn't do anything I commanded of him. Much to my embarrassed dismay, we went home empty handed that day. I never entered another dog show, but the training was not a total loss, because Muggs still performed well on our farm and was obedient until the end.

As Muggs grew into a mature dog, he developed bulging muscles that were rock hard. He was a ninety-pound dog with an appetite to match. It always astounded me at how quickly he could wolf down an immense quantity of dog food. It was a comical sight to see Muggs with his head down in the huge cast-iron frying pan that served as his dog dish. He was a loose-skinned dog, and, when he bent down, all the skin would pile up on his forehead in large folds. The frying pan was used as his dish, because it was the only one we had tried that could hold the vast amount of food and was heavy enough to stay in one spot while he ate it.

Not only was Muggs hilarious to look at with all his skin, but he was even more of a "leg-slapper" when one viewed him on the run. He obviously had fits trying to run, because he was so muscle bound. He would get going, full steam ahead, and then his back end would start to swing, first to one side, and then to the other. He also always ran at an angle and never straight ahead. The faster he ran, the more he'd get out of alignment, and then, without fail, one leg would catch up to the other leg, and Muggs would trip himself, only to go sprawling flat on his face.

Muggs always seemed like a gentle giant. He was tender with cats and even with little children tugging on his ears while he tried to sleep. The only time Muggs ever got the hot temper from his German shepherd blood, was when another male dog tried to set foot on our property. My first experience with this came when a large, stray, mongrel dog came to our farm one day. Without warning, the two dogs started fighting. Try as I would, I couldn't pull them apart. The other dog was bleeding in several places. By the time I could get Muggs off the stray, its front leg was hanging by only a few threads, and a large gaping slice on his neck was spurting blood. Dad put the dog out of its misery, but from then on we were careful about letting other dogs on our land.

One time I was glad that Muggs fought with another dog. The people who lived on the neighboring farm had a huge German shepherd. It had a terrible reputation for biting people around the area. One morning, my brother, Jerry, and I got up and went fishing at a pond on the other side of their property. We sneaked by ever so carefully and luckily went by undetected. After fishing, however, we were not quite so lucky. About halfway past the property, the dog came storming after us with fangs bared. I think Jerry and I could have set an olympic running record as we ran away. The dog kept coming though, and, just moments before we were sure we would have its gleaming teeth come sinking into the flesh of our legs, Muggs rounded the edge of our property to see what the commotion was.

The shepherd stopped and the two dogs' eyes met in an icy stare. As Muggs always did, he tore into that big dog with lightning grace and quickness. For a dog that couldn't run too well and slept most of the time, he sure could fight like a demon. Jerry and I just breathed a heavy sigh of relief and gleefully laughed as Muggs clasped a throat hold on the other dog and held on as the German shepherd tormentor ran dragging him down the road in yelping fear.

When the family brought Muggs home, he was given his own doghouse, right next to our house. Dad had had a friend build an enormous doghouse, and we always chained Muggs to it at night so he wouldn't roam the country, as many male dogs do. The strange part to me was that such a huge doghouse had such a small door in it. I asked Dad about it one day, and he explained that the small door prevented the cold from entering in the winter. Everyone would begin to laugh whenever Muggs tried to squeeze in or out of that little hole. How he ever made it through each day, I'll never know.

The older Muggs got, the more he loved to sleep. I always felt a little sorry for him in the winter, though, because, being a short-haired dog, he would shiver violently on a cold winter day. One morning, as I was doing some chores, I noticed something that wasn't normally a part of the roof on one of our chicken houses. As I drew closer, sure enough, it was Muggs stretched out on the peak of the roof "sawing logs." I gave him a call, and he jumped to his feet, then disappeared down the other side of the roof. I ran around to the other side and saw how the old sneak had done it. A large snowdrift had blown up against the building. Muggs must have figured that by making a bed out of the chicken house roof, he could lie in warm comfort for the rest of the winter, and that's just what he did, too.

Muggs was a part of our family for seven years of fun. No animal I had ever come in contact with had been more of a big, lovable dummy.

In comparison to the years and years that Tippy, our other dog, was on the farm, Muggs's life seemed a short one. Larger, more muscular dogs, like boxers, however, often live shorter lives than smaller dogs. The last summer we shared with Muggs was a different one. He became extremely arthritic and stiff. It almost hurt just to watch him walk, and he couldn't run anymore. Toward the end of summer, as the days got shorter and colder, Muggs would sometimes just lie and whine in pain. It seemed somehow cruelly pathetic to see our once noble friend in such misery. At last we decided that, for Muggs's sake he should be painlessly put to sleep by the veterinarian.

With the end of Muggs's life, so ends this story. Our farm has since had other dogs and other pets, but as with any true friend, Muggs's memories will forever linger.

9

○ ○ ○ ○

Polled Hereford Mania

Polled Hereford beef cattle have played a more significant, and lasting part in my upbringing than perhaps any other species of animal. I told, in my first chapter, how a horned, white-face bull was one of the first animals I can remember. From that time of my life, at age four, until present, I have had an incredible love for the white-face bovine called a Hereford.

To have an understanding of this breed of cattle, one must first gain some knowledge of their origin.

A first-class book was written in the 1970s by Orville Sweet, the past president of the American Polled Hereford Association of America. *The Birth of a Breed* was a book showing, in depth, this one breed of beef cattle. The book dealt not only with the origin of Polled Herefords, but also showed their struggles with climbing the ladder of success toward acceptance.

I will briefly try to outline some of the important aspects of the origin of this breed that Mr. Sweet so beautifully incorporated into his book.

Most people already know about the many famous components that made up the Old West. Obviously, the longhorn steer was as famous an animal in writing the history pages of the West as any other single aspect. One might ask what this had to do with Polled Herefords, but, with patience, I will show how history worked them into the picture.

The rugged longhorn, at one point in time, was most definitely the dominant breed of cattle. In time, however, the need for cattle that could ward off preying mountain lions, or cope with several-hundred-mile cattle drives subsided. The rather tough, stringy meat of the old longhorn began its trek to obscurity, as other breeds of beef cattle began coming on the scene.

One breed in particular that surfaced was the red, white-face Hereford cattle. It was as though nature had provided a compromise with this breed. Here was an animal that had enough horns on its head for ample protection for itself, was hardy enough to weather almost any extreme in environment, and yet was able to provide highly tender, tasty quantities of meat for the ice chest. Granted, many other breeds of beef also played important roles in our history, but I feel Hereford cattle were the main forerunners in this event.

The time scale of all that had taken place this far was during the 1800s. As the turn of the century came, once again other criteria were being analyzed in beef cattle. Hereford cattle were so numerous that they were seen all over our nation, perhaps in comparison to the American buffalo herds of a bygone time.

As the clocks turned into the twentieth century, a farmer named Gammon, from Iowa, decided to start an experiment with Hereford cattle. The year was 1901, and Mr. Gammon started working on a hunch he had felt. On a few occasions in his own herd of Hereford beef cattle, Mr. Gammon owned cows that occasionally gave birth to hornless calves. How odd the little genetic mutant calves must have looked next to their mothers, without the familiar set of horn stubs that kept getting larger and larger with the calf. Back in those times, these calves were eventually selected off and sent to market. Seldom were they used as a breeding stock, for fear of propagating their highly undesirable trait of hornlessness. It was believed that, without horns, a beef animal just lacked too much ruggedness. Mr. Gammon's hunch, however, if successful, was destined to change the philosophy of the entire beef industry.

After giving some thought to these hornless or polled calves, Mr. Gammon came to several conclusions. To begin with, the days of wild-animal attacks and roaming herds of cattle were all but gone from the face of the earth. Our nation was rapidly becoming more civilized, with less threat from wild animals than ever before. Farmers and ranchers were putting up fences and leaving their herds unattended now, rather than letting them "ride the range" as once had been done. Mr. Gammon felt if he could somehow start breeding to achieve this hornless or polled trait, he might have an innovative way of raising beef. To his way of thinking, the horns were, in fact, detrimental to the breed. No longer did the cattle have to defend themselves, and, whenever one had to work with horned cattle, the danger of the animal's ability to inflict human injury was always present. With feedlots of feeder cattle already springing up, the practice of cutting the horns off was becoming quite common. For these reasons, why not just raise a polled breed of cattle and be done with it?

Mr. Gammon sent letters out to Hereford breeders all across the nation inquiring about any polled Hereford calves that may have been born. From the replies, he had about fifteen hundred polled cattle to select from. After viewing them, Mr. Gammon felt that only eleven of these polled Herefords were of high enough quality to be the origin of a new breed.

Eventually Mr. Gammon's herd grew, and, after years of fending off sneers and derogatory comments, the breed began to take hold. Soon other breeders followed suit and started breeding and raising beef with this polled trait.

Genetics are often hard to understand, but the polled gene in cattle is a mutation from the horned gene. Even though the polled gene originates from the horned breed, it still is dominant. For this reason, one can breed a horned cow with a polled bull, and the resulting calf is generally polled.

Today, Polled Herefords are one of the largest breeds of beef cattle in the United States. The breed is now separated from the Hereford breed or horned Hereford cattle, and is not to be considered one and the same, even though both have similar markings.

With this small history lesson on Polled Hereford beef cattle, I can now return to my dealings with the breed and relate how these cattle have helped shape my life and the lives of my family members.

Almost within months from our arrival on our new farm, my father purchased a small herd of purebred Polled Hereford beef cattle to roam and graze the hilly pasture of our farm. Our original fifteen cows and one bull provided a picturesque view on the hill slope, as they contentedly grazed the warm summertime away. From the beginning, Jerry and I showed more than a blatant interest in the beef. We loved the springtime when new baby calves were born. So many times we would lie, stomach down, under the fence, with a long stem of fresh, tasty, springtime grass between our teeth, and watch a cow giving birth to her calf. We often would find ourselves grunting and breathing hard with each labor contraction the cow went through. First, one could see the small, white front feet.

Next a quivering little nose would protrude from underneath the laboring cow's tail. Then slowly, but surely, with mighty pushes, out the baby calf would pop. After a short gaining of her breath, the proud and protective mother would hop to her feet and provide the life-stimulating tongue-licking that has brought so many calves to life. Jerry and I would smile from ear to ear as the calf, within minutes, would be shaking its head about and trying to stand. Somehow, the shaking legs would provide enough support for the newborn to stand, but then they would give out and send the calf flopping harshly back to the hard ground. Eventually, though, in its battle for nourishment, the little beef calf would get up and make it to his mother's back end for some groceries. How I laugh to this day, each time I see a happy, contented calf wagging its tail from side to side as it nourishes itself.

Each spring, with the calving season over, our cows, calves, and bull were free to roam the pasture throughout the summer. My brother and I would often determine which calves were showing the most growth progress as the months went by. As summer turned to fall, the once-tiny beef calves had to be taken from their mothers and weaned. How amazing that a seventy-pound calf could grow into a five-hundred-pounder by just the start of fall.

All the calves were separated, with bull calves in one pen and heifers in another. As is still the case to this day, the next week always proves to be bearable only to someone wearing earplugs. One cannot imagine how many twenty-four hour-days in a row those grieving cows and disgusted calves could bellow their vocal cords out. Soon enough, though, the already-impregnated cows would forget their babies, and, likewise, the calves would soon find a feed bunk full of feed much more engrossing than standing by a fence and bawling.

One day, about three years after our start in the Polled Hereford business, my father started thinking of a new way of enjoying our beef.

"Scott and Jerry, how would you like to help me pick out a calf to show for the fair in August?" asked our father at the start of the summer.

"All right," came our quick reply in unison.

The unfortunate problem soon to surface was that no one in my family had ever been to a beef show. Jerry was only about five, and I was only nine years old, so our contributions in aiding Dad were minimal at best. At any rate, we dove into this project as father and sons bent on making a real project of it.

We went into our heifer lot and started deciding on the correct female to represent our farm. Because our beef herd was small in number we had only six yearling heifers to choose from.

"Okay, boys, which one do you think is the prettiest show animal?" asked Dad.

Jerry and I looked and looked with our untrained eyes for that prize-winning beef. Before long, the three of us had decided that Daisy was definitely the prettiest heifer in the lot.

We were to learn at our virgin attempt at showing in a few months that prettiness has little to do with a beef animal's qualities for the show ring. A judge makes his selection based on how large the frame is, both in length and height. He also evaluates the animal's straightness and correctness. As we found out all too harshly, Daisy was like a cute, extremely small, large-eyed, over fat mouse—compared with her competition.

Shortly after deciding Daisy would represent our herd at the Rochester fair, my father, brother, and I went to the owner of one of the larger Polled Hereford herds in the state and asked for some assistance. He outlined several steps involved in preparing an animal for show, such steps as trimming the hooves, clipping the hair, training the animal to lead and so forth. We thanked him for his help and departed to begin our task.

When August rolled around, we were ready for the show. Dad hired a truck to haul Daisy to town for our first open-class beef show. I must say we were very proud, and yet quite wide eyed, at the activities of the cattle barn. The expertise of the professionals within the building's walls was just amazing to Jerry and me. Not long after we arrived at the show, we came upon a cruel realization. The man we had put our trust in, to help us prior to the show, had evidently misinformed us on purpose. Dad had so carefully trimmed Daisy to the correct specifications. The problem, however, arose when we found out that one doesn't clip out the ears of a beef animal because the long hair helps make the animal look more rugged. One also doesn't shave the tail down to the skin, but rather leaves this long to help the animal look wider in the rear quarters. Imagine, if you will, how embarrassed we felt. To make matters worse, this man had told us to bring a cane to help square the legs of the heifer in the show ring. My Dad had bought a nice, curve-handled walking cane for use in the show ring. Once again we were demoralized when we viewed other exhibiters with special show sticks. The sticks consisted of a five-foot piece of wood with small hooks in the end. The idea was that one could poke one's animal in the legs to achieve the proper square stance and then use the small, hooked end to scratch its stomach. This gentle scratching helps keep the animal quiet and usually keeps him from moving around.

At the end of the day, my brother, father, and I went back home, extremely dejected. In a class of eighteen heifers, we had stood last. To make matters worse, I had heard someone in the crowd comment that if there had been another fifty animals, we still would have been last.

As I write this now, the humility I saw in my father's eyes, as he was being laughed at, still hurts me. Sometimes it is hard to understand how people can be so cruel, especially when someone is trying his best. I remember walking into Daisy's pen the night after that horrifying show and crying with my small arms wrapped tightly around her neck.

This could have been the end of our show-ring appearances. Under the trying circumstances, few people would have ever braved another chance at such torment. My strong father, though, was even more determined to get the final laugh.

The next year, the three of us once again were back in the heifer lot, evaluating a new crop of yearling heifers. The main advantages for us this time were more built-in determination and a hundred percent more experience than we had had the year before. This time, two heifers were selected for the upcoming show. We progressed through the summer working hard with them, and before long we were again at the fair. Once again the evasive prize-winner evaded our grasp, but Dad and I stood seventh and eighth, in a class of fourteen animals. There were definitely fewer jeers this go-round, and we went home with our heads held much higher.

The third year, we came back for yet another round. On this attempt we stilled the laughter for good, as we came home with our first Grand Champion purple ribbon.

Many different Polled Hereford bulls and heifers have left their mark on my memory. Many of them have exhibited remarkably interesting personalities.

I remember all too well our big herd bull. His name was Superol. Polled Hereford bulls are notorious for their passiveness, and seldom has there ever been a mean or dangerous one. Superol did show me some new respect though.

On our farm, the normal turn of events went something like this. The cows were in their lot all winter, and the bull had a special pen by himself. The reason for this is that, when the cows start calving, one doesn't want the bull mating with the cows until the proper time has come. When spring rolled around that year, we turned the cow herd and their calves out to pasture. Superol, however, had to stay in his little pen, and he longed to be with his girls. The sight of their freedom definitely wasn't sitting well with the big bull.

As was always the case, in a few weeks Superol was allowed his freedom. Dad opened the gate, and off the bull ran, frolicking and kicking his heels as though he were a young calf. The problem was that the cows were on the south end of the pasture, and Superol ran to the north end. Dad told me to run out quickly and direct Superol back to the cows. I was about eleven at the time and knew bulls were to be respected, but Superol was surely no problem.

Out to the pasture I ran, while Dad looked on from the barn. As I drew near to Superol, I tried to chase him toward the cow herd, but he spun around and started bellowing. I remember thinking, "Holy cow!" and took off, running. I was about fifty yards from a big oak tree in the pasture, and I headed straight for it. Right on my heels came the bull. I just made it to the tree, and that crazy bull started chasing me around it. Around and around we went. Dad was sitting up at the barn just rolling on the ground laughing, and I was screaming at the top of my lungs for help. I wanted so badly to be tall enough to crawl into the tree, but there was no way, so around and around the tree he chased me. When I could hardly go anymore, a cow let out an enticing call from the distance, and off the bull ran. I trembled my way back to my father, who by now was getting a terrible side ache from his laughter. I "cussed him out good" for laughing. We both agreed that Superol probably had not liked the thought of being bothered so shortly after having been set free, and this had caused the problem. I'm still not sure if he was really mad that day or just playing with me and trying to use up some of his excess energy. I can tell you one thing, though, and that is, when two thousand pounds of bull wants to play with my little body, I'm going to run every time.

This brings me to a highly personal story about a heifer that really changed the lives of my family. Her reputation was spread so far that I was asked many years ago to write about her life story in a nationally distributed youth magazine called the *Winners Way*.

It all started in the fall of 1971. After showing our Polled Herefords on a small scale for a few years, and with only a few cattle to pick good show prospects from, my father, brother, and I decided to expand our beef operation. The most inexpensive route was to purchase young replacement females and then raise them, ourselves, into cows.

An opportunity arose when Don Richmond, from the Royal Oaks Ranch, put some of his excess cattle up for sale. Don had offered several breeders in the area a chance to buy four half-sisters he had purchased himself in another sale. With no one wanting to take a chance on these heifers, Don had asked my family if we would be interested. We debated for some time on whether to take the gamble ourselves. It seemed as though they were quite small for their age, and Dad was sure they were smaller than our own heifers at home.

We did, however, purchase them, and, to our dismay, they were in fact smaller than even our tiniest heifer. All that was left was to accept the mistake of buying the heifers and try to raise them so they could one day be cows. The group of beef females was fed a grower ration once in the morning and once at night. This ration consisted mainly of oats, some corn, with small parts of molasses for taste appeal, salt, minerals, linseed meal for coat shine, and bran for healthy digestion.

Along with all this, they got a few pounds of alfalfa to meet their roughage needs.

As winter evolved into spring, to our astonishment, all four of the heifers we'd bought had caught up in size with our own, home-raised ones. One heifer, in fact, looked even a little larger than our own.

At the start of the summer, I picked out the possible animals for our show string. One of the four was, by this time, quite far ahead of the rest. This heifer, whose registered name was GHF Lady Dom 1, became like a pet in the family. Soon everyone was calling her by her nickname, Baby Heifer.

Her first step toward the show season involved teaching her to lead and to set her legs squarely. No matter how patient I tried to be, she tested my patience constantly by kicking and acting wild. I think there are still a couple show sticks around the farm that were bent on her head through impatient disgust.

When she was finally trained to lead, we began working her hair. The whole philosophy is that the longer one can grow a beef animal's coat, the more one can use it to make the animal look more presentable to a judge. Toward the end of the show season, Jerry and I were brushing this heifer as much as four hours per day. Working her hair also included wetting her down frequently. With the brushing stimulating growth and the cooling effect of the water, even during the summer, Baby Heifer's hair grew like crazy. One can imagine, though, how all this excess attention started turning her into a spoiled heifer.

For our first show, we chose a small fair. When it was over, Baby Heifer had won her first Grand Champion honors. I thought how terrific this was, considering she had been bought only for replacement purposes. Little were we to know that in the following two years of showing, this heifer would win enough purple ribbons to wallpaper a room with and pay herself off twofold just in premium money.

The more we showed Baby Heifer, the more Jerry, Dad; and I expanded our knowledge. The first five shows, we were still such novices at showing that we really didn't realize how good she was. By the end of this beef heifer's two-year show-ring career, we had all graduated into the big leagues of showing cattle. Baby Heifer was shown in several states, and she put her prize-winning stamp in each one.

During the show season, my father, brother, and I always take up permanent residence in the cattle barns. Our beds are usually cots or some bales of straw and sleeping bags. Often, during a long day at a fair, the three of us used to fall sound asleep in the straw next to Baby Heifer, as she contentedly chewed her cud.

Each time before we led Baby Heifer into a new show arena, I would stroke her neck and whisper in her ear, "Okay, Baby Heifer, one more Grand Champion, and you can go back home." All Baby Heifer ever did was act bored with the whole process.

Baby Heifer ended her show career with an incredible record of sixteen Grand Champion and three Reserve Champion honors.

This fantastic beef female is still in our herd, and, as one might expect, is our best cow. Thanks to Baby Heifer, my family had the opportunity to broaden its horizons and achieve many goals. We were once told that seldom is any beef producer lucky enough to find an animal like her during a lifetime. It was certainly our sincere hope that someday she could produce a calf like herself, and we could try to set the world on fire again.

Baby Junior was a heifer calf born purely by chance. As one might have expected, Baby Heifer certainly did produce a calf with true show-ring qualifications.

For the first few years of raising offspring, though, Baby Heifer produced above-average calves, but none had the Grand Champion potential of their dam. The biggest problem was that we just didn't own a bull that could mate with this cow and improve her qualities. Finally, Jerry and I bought a bull from a breeder in Florida, and then the champions started being born. This bull was a huge, gentle giant that weighed in at two thousand three hundred pounds. He was as straight and correct as one could find anywhere. His first mating on our farm was Baby Heifer, and her resulting calf was something to view.

Right from the start, Junior had long, colt like legs, a beautiful, feminine head, and above-average dimensions. Dad commented each and every day that he had never seen anything like her before. As she frolicked through the pasture, Junior knew she was far better than any other calf. By the time fall was turning the leaves from green to all colors of the rainbow, we felt our "pot of gold" had been found.

At weaning time, Junior outweighed our bull calves, which is difficult for a heifer to do. Even her height measurements were inches above the others. Jerry and I commented that she was so far ahead of what Baby Heifer had been at that age that it was almost hard to believe. Dad was quick to mention, however, that Baby Heifer's results still hung on our walls in the form of many ribbons and trophies. He informed us that Junior would have to grow tremendously to ever be what her mother had been.

Junior went into the heifer lot with the others and went through the familiar bawling for days on end. Before long, all the young stock happily chewed down their grain, and their memories of mama were fading.

With January approaching, my father decided to try an almost-unheard-of task. This task was to prepare Junior for the National Polled Hereford Show in Fort Worth, Texas. Why such an unheard of task, one might ask. The problem was that almost all calves who are shown at about six or seven months of age in a national show either come from the southern states or are heavily pampered prior to the show. Minnesota calves must often face severe weather and generally have few hopes of winning anything as calves especially before they make it through their first winter. Junior was certainly not being pampered and was outside fighting the blizzards in the same fashion as the other calves.

No amount of discussing on my part would alter my father's decision. I should make point of the fact that I was in college at this time. For two years, I had been working under Dr. Charles Christians on the University of Minnesota livestock judging team. I firmly felt with all my experience from my animal science degree and with the judging teamwork, I should have had some say in the whole matter.

Dad eventually had Jerry on his side, and they just kept repeating how good Junior was. Jerry was going to take Junior to the show himself, since I was in school and Dad had to run the farm. As my brother loaded the heifer into the truck and readied himself for the trip to Texas, I wished him luck. I felt more than ever he would need luck.

The following week we all waited for the phone to ring. Dad was still optimistic, and I held strongly to my pessimistic views. I remember thinking how glad I was not to have to have had to go through the embarrassment of being last in class again after all these years of doing so well. Once again, though, I will point out my feeling. I knew Junior was exceptional but felt she just didn't stand a chance against the nation's best calves. My hopes were for her to be the best yearling in the country during the following year.

One afternoon the phone finally rang, with an operator saying, "Collect call from Jerry in Texas. Will you accept the charges?"

"Yes!" returned my anxious father.

I ran to another phone, since I was home temporarily for a visit. "Dad, Scott, you'll never believe this."

"What happened?" we jointly yelled over the phone.

Jerry went on to explain how he had taken Junior into the show arena, with close to forty other calves. When the class placing was over, he had stood in third spot. Now, maybe that doesn't sound like much of an accomplishment, but, to us, that news was like man's first step on the moon. While I was still trying to close my gaping mouth, Jerry went on.

"There are two separate ranchers from down south that want to buy Junior. They look like the millionaire type to me. They each offered me ten thousand dollars. What should I do?"

Silence . . . .

"Dad, what should I do?" Jerry repeated.

Silence . . . .

Finally Dad came out of his trance and started stuttering away. He said how we certainly needed the money to make some farm payments. None of us could comprehend the huge amount of money being spoken of. Until that point in time, the most expensive heifer we had ever sold was for about six hundred dollars.

Dad's sorrowful decision was to sell Junior. His feelings were that Baby Heifer was still young enough that she could raise another calf just like Junior.

I could sense Jerry's disappointment along with mine, even though he and I were separated by over a thousand miles of telephone wires.

All of a sudden Dad shouted, "The hell with it. If they think she's worth that much, then it's worth a try to see how well we can show her around the country."

"Good decision," Jerry and I chimed in.

Dad and I wished Jerry a safe trip back home and hung up.

When Junior returned to Minnesota, I assure you, she was treated like a queen. We took special care of her, and she was brought along for the upcoming show season, much as her mother had been in the previous years.

The first show of the summer seemed to come on so suddenly, but off went Junior to another national show in Springfield, Illinois. Again, the evasive champion ribbon was unclaimed by Junior, but she was first place in her class and eventually helped my brother win the first place National Showmanship honors.

The following months were filled with joy and happiness for my dad, my brother, and me. Each show Junior participated in, she would stamp out her competition one by one. The most difficult fact to cope with was that Junior, as only a late yearling, was already larger than her prizewinning dam. Even so, a show was seldom ever "in the bag," due to the fact that the animals being shown were of more quality than in Baby Heifer's day. This was certainly the results of true genetic improvement within the Polled Hereford breed of cattle.

State fair after state fair fell to Junior, as purple ribbons and premium money came in. Everything was going well for us. Then we went to the Iowa State Fair.

Junior was still growing like a weed, and, by this time, seldom was there a doubt as to the overall winner of a fair. The night before the Iowa show, Jerry and I bedded our heifer and then went to bed early, because we were to start washing at three o'clock in the morning. When morning arrived, we dressed and went to start our chores. To our disbelief, there stood Junior with a huge, gaping pitchfork wound in her back leg. She was bleeding profusely, and her leg was swollen to twice its normal size. Obviously, she could put no weight on her leg. There was no doubt some devilish person had purposely inflicted this injury on our poor animal, simply in hope of causing her defeat with the painful wound.

If one could have seen the pain in Junior's large, brown eyes! Here was a sweet, innocent animal with no malice for anyone or anything. Yet some cruel, heartless idiot was able to do such a terrible thing.

The first matter to take care of was to call a veterinarian. Within minutes, a vet was by Junior's side, examining the wound. We pleaded with him to find a way to get her to walk in time for the early-morning show. After stopping the bleeding, the vet asked if Junior was pregnant. We confirmed that she was with calf about three months. Adding to our agony, he informed us of a painkiller he could inject into her system, but the side effects would cause her to abort the calf. I battled with the decision, but finally told him to give her the shot. My hopes were not only to stop the pain, but also to make her feel well enough for the show.

As the show time rolled around, the drug had done little to stop the pain in her leg. We therefore had to show her with only three legs capable of supporting her weight. In a few days, Junior did abort her calf, and this further fired our fury, since the drug had not actually taken effect on her pain until after the show.

In any event, Junior limped into the ring that day and was eventually crowned Grand Champion. I still vividly remember Judge Don Riffle saying, "I know this heifer wasn't born with that injury, and I think she's just too damn good to beat." The Grand Champion decision took great courage on his part, because it's a well-known fact that beef cattle must be selected for their soundness of feet and legs, due to the large range land they often must cover.

Junior went on from Iowa and continued in her winning ways. She eventually beat the two animals that had placed above her at the first show of her career in Texas. Jerry, Dad, and I went from show to show, much as we always had. Somehow, though, a little bit of us had died back at the Iowa fair. Our total trust and faith in mankind had been tested. We learned that some people have no bounds on how low they will stoop in their own quest for victory. I'll never forgive that person, whoever it was, for doing the insensitive action of wounding a defenseless animal, just to hurt another human being.

The time came when Junior was retired from competition and put out to the same pasture as Baby Heifer. What a sight to see these two magnificent females, mother and daughter, proudly eyeing their calves and grazing the green slopes. In viewing them, one could hardly wait to see which would produce the next Grand Champion.

10

o o o o

The Process
Goes On and On

Three years without a pony or horse on the farm had elapsed, and I was certainly getting the itch to ride again. After all, what horse-loving, sixteen-year-old lad wouldn't have had the itch? Until now, Dad had just been getting subtle hints as to my equine desires, but more intensive action was due. No doubt, Dad realized how badly I wanted a horse, but the financial problems of the farm at the time just wouldn't allow for my exigencies. My folks were still feeling the repercussions of their economically disastrous poultry endeavor. For this reason, little money was ever available for extra luxuries. Not wanting to put further burden on my family, I let the topic drop.

Shortly thereafter, our neighbors acquired an interesting animal. Dick and Della were farmers like my parents. They had a friend who lived in town, and this friend wanted to board his mare on Dick's farm. This so excited me, I could hardly be controlled when I heard the news. I figured the next best situation to owning one's own horse was to have one next door.

The first day I saw Gypsy in the neighboring pasture, elation was my innermost feeling. Gypsy was a big, brown-colored mare with tender eyes and a gentle manner. I spent more than a few hours stroking her smooth, glistening neck. Having the friendly mare next door was a temporary resolution of my desire for a horse, but, before long, the feelings crept back.

Gypsy was no substitute for my own horse. I enjoyed spending time with her, but I wasn't even allowed to ride her. Whenever possible, though, and provided no one was looking, I would hop up on her back; then, with my hands clasped tightly in Gypsy's long mane, off we would go, riding bareback. Eventually my elation for Gypsy reverted to depression, as I once again longed for my own horse.

Dick informed me one afternoon that Gypsy was pregnant and going to foal in a couple of months. This was great news, but the best was about to come. Dick said he and Gypsy's owner had come to an agreement. Since the owner didn't want another horse, he had made a deal with Dick. In payment for Gypsy's board, Dick and Della could keep the upcoming foal. Dick told me he had a proposition that might interest me. With all ears open, I let him progress.

"Since you've really shown how much you like horses, Della and I have decided we would sell the foal to you if you want," Dick announced.

"Hey, Dick, that's the best news I've ever heard!" came my reply.

All of a sudden, a horrible thought crossed my mind. Just because this foal was going to only be walking distance away didn't change my financial picture. I only had a sum total of seventy dollars to my name, and I knew Mom and Dad wouldn't be too happy to assist me at this time. Dick had not quoted a price, but I knew all too well the expensive dollars it took to buy even a baby horse.

"Gee, Dick, I want that foal real bad, but I only have seventy bucks," I sadly replied.

"I'll tell you what. If you do chores on our farm once in a while when Della and I go on vacation, I'll let you have the foal for seventy dollars," said Dick.

I gleefully told him, "You've got yourself a deal."

Now, just as it had been when I was younger and owned my own pony, I counted each minute of the long days waiting for the newborn. After what seemed an eternity, Dick called me one morning and told me to run across the road to see my newborn foal. I'd almost bet I was in their yard before the receiver on the telephone came to rest.

There before me was a long-legged, wide-eyed, little filly foal nursing from her mother. She was chestnut in color with two white socks on her hind feet, and a petite strip of white running down her forehead. I'd already decided on the name of Dixie if the foal was a female.

Right from the first day of her life, Dixie knew what extensive attention was. Dad often pestered me about how we would sure be glad when Dixie was weaned and on our farm, so he'd be able to see me once in a while.

As soon as my little filly started trusting me, I set right to work training her. As usual, time went quickly, and I knew in only a few months she would have to be taken from her mother and brought to our farm.

I purchased a cute, tiny halter for Dixie, so her leading lessons could begin. Did I laugh as I put the halter on her for the first time! Dixie's eyes got large and mistrusting. When the leather contraption was in place, off she ran to Lola, whinnying in her high-pitched style and shaking her head all about.

After letting a couple of days go by for Dixie to adjust to her halter, I was ready to begin the laborious task of training her to lead.

As was the case with training my pony to lead, so it was with Dixie, with a tug of war between man and beast. Odd, however, was the fact I had been smaller and younger when training the smaller pony. Now, a few years later, I was larger, but now I was training a larger foal. The way it worked out, I was still at no advantage in size or strength.

Della would watch from the fence and laugh as Dixie pulled from the end of rope fastened to her halter, and I pulled from my end. In the beginning, I thought Dixie was going to end up training me to lead, because I certainly went more in her direction than she did in mine. It's not easy trying to out traction an animal when it's got four-wheel drive and a person only two-wheel drive. In time, however, Dixie's chin began getting sore—not to mention my blistered hand—and she started making the familiar choppy hops forward. With some reward and patting on the neck, Dixie soon learned to follow willingly with a gentle tug on her halter.

The time finally arrived when I paid Dick my seventy dollars and led Dixie across the road to our farm. Dad and I had spent a great deal of time building a nice, white wooden fence around the building that was to be Dixie's home. Horses can often badly injure themselves on barbed-wire fences, so I would have nothing but the best for my filly. Once in her new home, Dixie carried on quite extensively for a few days, as she got used to being without her mother. Finally, she quieted down, and I began my next phase of training.

I already realized that the two years it would take for Dixie to be old enough to ride would be a long time. For this reason, I had decided to spend the time training my horse to do tricks. Mom had purchased a book for my birthday called *Horse Tricks,* and I quickly read it from cover to cover. I envisioned owning the world's most intelligent horse, a horse that could do any trick. With these thoughts still in my mind, I began the lessons.

The first trick was teaching Dixie to shake hands, or hoofs, if one prefers. All that was required was the standard procedure one teaches when training a dog to shake. It simply involved repeatedly lifting the animal's front leg up, shaking it, setting it down, and then rewarding the animal with either some type of appealing food, or else just a rewarding pat on the head or neck. Sure enough, before much time at all, Dixie would happily thrust her front leg forward on command and shake with anyone.

The next trick involved teaching Dixie to say yes and no. More descriptively, to shake her head yes or no. Once again, a simple philosophy was involved, with a reward upon achievement. One simply took a pin or needle in his hand. After asking the horse a yes or no question, one made a definite motion to either the side of the horse's neck or underneath its chest, and gently pricked the horse in that spot. The idea was to make the horse think the slight prick of the needle was a fly biting it. Dixie would poke her nose either to the side on a no question, or downward on a yes question. Each time, I would reward her. In no time at all, the prick of the pin was no longer necessary, because only a slight movement of my hand to either the side of her neck or toward her chest would send her into a yes or no demonstration. This method of training was not cruel or inhumane, because it really didn't harm Dixie at all; in fact she actually loved all the attention. The real trick is the demonstration to someone else; one had to ask questions and just use one's hands while talking. To the onlooker, it appeared as though he was witnessing a most extraordinary horse.

For my last trick, I taught Dixie kissing. Again, one simply commands the horse to kiss and then holds something like a sugar cube to one's chin. The horse reaches out, takes the cube, and is affectionately rewarded. With enough repetition, the horse reaches out to kiss just for the neck-stroking afterward.

At this point, I was running out of time to train Dixie, so she was left with the ability to do three tricks. These tricks, though, were more than enough to make her extremely popular with all my friends and with all the neighbors.

Even though I had abandoned my desire of training her to roll over, play dead, kneel, and so forth, I greatly enjoyed demonstrating the tricks Dixie could do. I later found out, if one doesn't keep up with the learned tricks, a horse soon forgets. After the novelty of these tricks wore off, I eventually stopped doing any of them except the shaking. Dixie never forgot how to shake hands, but, in time, she could no longer remember how to kiss or say yes and no. I just never bothered to retrain her, either.

I'll never forget the time she cut her front leg badly on a jagged piece of steel. I called the veterinarian out immediately to look Dixie over. The vet actually got upset, because, even though she was in extreme pain, Dixie would lift up her badly injured leg to shake hands each time the vet stooped down to look at the wound. Eventually, however, the vet took care of her cut, and she healed well.

When the following spring arrived, Dixie was one year old and developing into a fine young horse. My problem was that there was still no horse to ride, as Dixie was yet too young. I once again began pestering my poor father for another horse. The previous year had been a financially successful year on the farm, so he finally said he'd see what he could do.

Dad didn't waste much time, because, within a couple of weeks, a horse trailer pulled in the yard. My father always gets such a sparkle in his eyes when he can pull off a sneaky trick and then watch the enjoyment that trick can bring. Enjoyment was not the word for my feeling when I saw the huge, bay-colored mare unloaded from the trailer. The mare had a silky, smooth, brown hair coat, with a lovely black mane and tail. Dad quickly told me how he had acquired her.

On the east side of the city of Rochester lived a friend of my father's. Dad said he owned a registered American Standardbred mare that had been professionally raced as a harness horse in her younger days. The friend's children no longer used the mare anymore, and therefore the chance for my father's purchase arose. The mare's name was Sunday Queen and even at ten years of age, she still looked every bit the part of a racehorse.

After almost kissing my father's feet for doing such a generous and loving deed, I set off to saddle up my latest four-legged beast. In only minutes, Queen and I set off across the field for a good long run, a run by horseback that I'd been craving for years now. At first, we set out at a walk. Queen's long legs provided a nice, easy pace. With a slight prod to her ribs, we sped to a trot. Let me tell you, what a trot it was! As a professional trotting, harness horse, she had raced many times, and I couldn't believe her pace. I'd never been on a horse before that could go so fast in a trot. Queen was almost as smooth as sitting on a chair. This struck me as odd, since generally the trot is a horse's most choppy gait. In any event, I prodded her once again, so we could proceed into a swift, breakneck gallop. To my astonishment, she continued trotting. Once again I prodded her harder with my heels, and, stubbornly, Queen gave no response. I continued my urging until I didn't have any more strength to prod her. I dejectedly turned the mare for home, unable to understand what was wrong with this horse.

At home, Dad explained Queen had been bred and raised to be a trotter. On the racetrack, if a horse breaks stride or goes from a trot to a gallop, the animal is disqualified from the race. Often when these horses did break stride, they were severely reprimanded to prevent any such further actions. Queen's trainer must have certainly done an excellent job, because she hadn't been on a track for years, and yet she refused to break stride.

Knowing the reason now, I decided there was little I could do but accept what was. It was terribly disappointing for me not to be able to run with the wind, but Queen was a beautiful horse, and I did appreciate her. Just to be able to ride the fields and woods of the countryside sent me into feverish ecstasy.

One day a high-school friend of mine named Steve brought his horse over, and we went riding. As we peacefully moved down the road, we discussed many interesting topics. The only one I actually remember, though, was girls. At that stage of our lives, girls were beginning to be awfully heavy considerations.

Before long, Steve wanted to race. I told him Queen wouldn't gallop, but he persisted. Steve said she might gallop if his horse did. I thought the idea was surely worth the try. Steve took off on his horse, and I nudged Queen to pursue. To our surprise, Queen took off at a tremendously fast trot and just about kept up with Steve's horse, who was galloping. It was then I realized she must have been fast in her racing days to be able to keep up with a horse traveling at a supposedly faster gait. Try as I might, though, Queen refused to break stride. Steve won the race, but Queen and I came in at a close second.

In about two months, I was quickly becoming unhappy with a horse that wouldn't go faster than a trot. It was embarrassing for me to ride with friends and not be able to gallop. Sure, I was proud of Queen, since she was a nice-looking horse and past racer at that, but she just didn't provide me with all the essentials necessary to satisfy my needs. I had promised myself, however, not to complain to Dad, because I knew this would hurt him deeply. After all what kind of uncaring little brat would I have been if I had not totally appreciated my father's gift?

One day, the phone rang for my father, and he talked quietly on it for a while, and then hung up. He headed toward me with a dismal look on his face, but my father was about to answer my prayers with his next words.

"Scott, I hate to say this to you, but Queen's old owners want her back."

"What for?" came my surprised reply.

"Evidently, their children really miss Queen now that she's not there anymore, and they want to know if they could possibly buy her back. I know that's just not fair, but they are my good friends. Of course, the decision is yours." said Dad.

"I wouldn't want their kids to be unhappy, Dad, so I guess it will be all right, but I hope I can get another horse," I told him with as depressing a look as I could muster up, quite at odds with my bubbling happiness inside.

Dad assured me we would both look for another horse to satisfy me until Dixie was old enough to ride. On the trailer Queen went, and off again she rode to her old home. As Queen left, I felt happy that she could go back to a place where she evidently was thoroughly appreciated. I was also glad for the chance to experience her most unique qualities.

My father and I came across an ad in the paper one day, advertising a quarterhorse gelding for sale. Dad and I drove to the farm the horse was at and looked him over. It was like "love at first sight." The gelding was sorrel in color and had the most beautiful head I'd ever seen on a horse. He had long, powerful legs, muscular hindquarters, and a bulging chest. After riding him, I quickly told Dad this was the horse we'd been scouting for.

I named him Toby, and he took up residence with Dixie on our farm. Toby was well mannered, since he had been shown in many horse shows. Toby and I were a perfect team from the start. The big horse loved being ridden, and I loved to ride him. I learned immediately after riding him for the first time what a speed demon he was. The first time I nudged him to check his galloping ability he thrust forward so fast I almost fell out of the saddle. Once he was at his top speed, I could hardly believe how fast the ground was speeding by.

The quarterhorse was bred for working cattle out West. It was bred with powerful hindquarters to give it an ability to start faster than any other breed of horse. This advantage allowed the quarterhorse to quickly take pursuit of a speeding beef animal. The quarterhorse also was bred for short, quick bursts of speed. The horse was given its name because not even a racing thoroughbred horse can beat a quarterhorse in a quarter-mile run. These horses were also bred with powerful builds, so a cowboy could rope a beef animal and his horse could withstand the pull of the cattle.

Toby was definitely no exception to any of the rules on how the quarterhorse had been bred. Shortly after receiving Toby, I entered him in the gaming division of a horse show. Since this was our first time at a show together, I entered him in a fun game called the "bat race." The race involves running one's horse into an arena with a baseball bat at the far end. Once at the bat, someone takes the horse while the contestant jumps to the ground, puts his chin to one end of the bat, and the other end of the bat on the ground, then spins. Around and around one must twirl—ten times to be exact. With this step completed, one must then dizzily stagger to the horse, try to get back in the saddle, and race back to the finish line in the shortest time.

It was hilarious to watch some of the contestants finish twirling, around the bats and then go staggering in the wrong direction from their horses. Oftentimes, the people couldn't even put their feet in the saddle when they did find their horses. Other times, their horses would go scampering away in fright at the strange actions of their masters.

Toby and I had set out to win a trophy at our first show, so, when our turn arrived, off we sped. Toby's speed brought us to the bat in no time. Off I jumped, and in seconds I was spinning the bat around. After ten twirls, I headed for Toby. Once at his side, I grabbed the saddle horn, put one foot in the stirrup, and off Toby flew. I wasn't completely in the saddle until we had almost crossed the finish line, but we won the event and set a new speed record for the "bat race."

I don't think I'd ever been more proud than winning that first trophy with Toby. In the following years, Toby and I won many other events at horse shows, but the most memorable was definitely our first event.

The more I rode Toby, the more I realized his love for running. He often acted as though his favorite part of our ride was when I'd let him "open up." Toby's neck would stretch forward, his tail would fly back, and his powerful strides would bring us along at tremendous speeds. It wasn't until I was riding again one day with my friend Steve that I realized just how fast my horse was. Steve once more challenged me to a race, and this time I confidently accepted. In unison, we both urged our horses forward, and immediately Toby was several paces ahead. Within moments, we were flying away from Steve and his horse. In total disbelief, I brought my hardly panting horse to a stop and pondered on his true racing potential.

Thanks to Steve, word of Toby's incredible speed spread throughout my school. Many nights were spent with Toby and me being challenged by some other kid and his horse. The result was always the same, with Toby blasting the challengers to bits.

Even Glen, my uncle, couldn't believe Toby's speed. One day Glen brought out his part bred mustang horse named Prince to challenge Toby and me. Prince, like Toby, had never been defeated in a race. In front of Glen's family and mine we raced not once, but three times! Glen said the first time he hadn't gotten a fair start. The second time I won, he claimed Prince hadn't liked running on a strange road. At last, after I had defeated him for a third time in one of my father's fields, Glen stated, "Scott, that is the fastest horse I've ever come across."

Finally, after approximately fifty undefeated races, I decided to enter Toby in the big race at our county fair a few months away. To my dismay, I broke my leg at the start of the summer and had to wear a cast for two months. I had already entered Toby and paid the entry fee, but I sadly came to the conclusion I'd be unable to race my horse in August. Even if the cast were off in time, two months of no exercise would leave Toby overweight and slow.

As I hobbled around the farm on crutches, I watched in amazement as Toby seemingly trained himself all summer for the big race. I'd never seen a horse that loved running so much. Toby and Dixie both were in the big cattle pasture. Each day Toby would run from end to end as fast as he could. Dixie would just watch with total disenchantment as the big gelding ran and ran. Sure enough, one week prior to the big race at the fair, my cast was removed. I gleefully started riding my horse again. Dad was extremely upset with me when he found out I was going to ride in the race. He informed me that I could hardly walk yet, and, if an accident happened during the race, I might rebreak my leg or even be killed. Nothing anyone could say, though, would deter me from my final goal with Toby.

Once at the fair, I saddled Toby and prepared him for the race. I suddenly realized I probably had bitten off more than I could chew at this race. Most of the other horses around me were saddled with lightweight, racing saddles. The people who were riding these horses were a lot lighter and small than I. The only saddle I owned was a large, heavy, Western, roping saddle. I heard many cruel comments from behind my back. People thought I was sure a dumb fool to bring a big, slow-looking horse into this reputable race. Some of the people actually laughed outright at me when they saw my saddle. I was rapidly losing my trace of confidence as I looked at the many racy-looking horses, including thoroughbreds all about Toby and me.

There were to be several different races that day, but I had entered Toby in the quarter-mile race. Dad was still raving about how foolish I was to race in my condition. At last we were called to the starting line. There were twelve horses in the race. Toby and I were positioned second from the inside rail. The flag went up and came down, and the race began. To my horrified surprise, the two horses on either side of Toby had squeezed together at the start and blocked off his usual speedy takeoff. Toby picked up speed and, almost with a vengeance, went blasting between the two horses in front of us. The horse on the inside was a black thoroughbred, and it maintained about a half-horse lead on Toby all around the turn of the track. The rest of the pack was quickly fading, but our race wasn't over yet. I never once kicked or swatted Toby as the other rider was doing to his horse because I knew my horse was giving everything he had. Toby always tried his best and probably had more will to win than I. For these reasons, I knew nothing I could do would help speed him up. As we turned into the straightaway with the finish line in sight, Toby laid his ears back and pushed forward. Ever so slowly, he inched forward on the black horse. By this time the crowd was standing and screaming. Just yards from the finish Toby overtook the thoroughbred and won the race by a neck.

When we came to a halt, I could have loved Toby to death. My father came running to my side, all excited. Jerry told me later that, when I headed for the starting line at the beginning of the race, Dad had said he wasn't even going to watch my foolishness. Once I started the race and we were neck and neck, Jerry said Dad suddenly was screaming the loudest of anyone at the race. I bet you'll never guess who did the most bragging about Toby and me winning the race, either.

I have to admit, Dixie did take a back seat to Toby that first year. Toby seemed as though he could do no wrong. Once I took him on a three-day trail ride. A trail ride is a get-together of many horse-lovers. The normal day consists of riding about twenty miles of rough terrain by horseback. One can imagine how exhausted a horse can get after a full day of this, much less three days in a row. As everyone else's horse began playing out and showing fatigue, Toby kept looking and acting fresher and fresher.

No one could believe how my horse was still acting as if he wanted to run a race by the end of the third day.

Soon after I acquired Toby, I started using him on our beef cattle. I often used his speed to help me chase the animals into the corral. At other times, I worked Toby like a bulldozer for pulling. One time Dad wanted to move a big fourteen-hundred-pound cow across our farm and put her in another area. We quickly realized she wasn't about to go. I threw a rope around the cow's neck, attached the rope to the saddle, and urged Toby forward. When he reached the end of the rope, he stopped, looked back and probably tried to figure out how to pull a cow that outweighed him by two hundred pounds. I prodded him again, and Toby leaned forward with all his might. The stubborn cow took one dragging step forward, then another, and another, until Toby, exhaustedly, had dragged her to the desired location.

On another occasion, our big beef bull in the pasture created some problems. Dad wanted to put the bull away for the winter, but he wouldn't come up from the pasture. The difficult problem was that the bull had positioned himself on the other side of the creek and wouldn't let anyone chase him across. I decided to bring Toby into the picture. Toby and I headed the bull toward the creek, but, instead of crossing, he took off like a bullet alongside of the water. Toby took off in hot pursuit. We went all along the creek but couldn't persuade the bull to cross over. Once again, the bull sped off along the creek. Finally, I lost my patience. While Toby was keeping pace on the outside of the bull, I quickly jerked Toby's reins, which sent the big horse smacking into the side of the beef bull. With a tremendous splash, the bull hit the water, and hurriedly climbed the bank on the other side to escape the horrible horse. I began laughing so hard I almost fell out of the saddle. Toby had once again proved his value to me.

Dixie's level of maturity finally reached the point at which she could be taught to ride. I swear, Dixie actually enjoyed this training period, because, for once, she was getting more attention than Toby. Dixie had always been exceptionally smart, and this time didn't prove to be any different. After giving her a slight adjustment period to get used to the saddle, I climbed upon her back for the first time. With Dad and Jerry watching on, Dixie gave three mild bucks and then started riding perfectly. Within a few weeks, she was riding so nicely that Dad and I went on our first trail ride together.

Now, it has never been a secret to anyone who knows my father, how much he dislikes horses. Dad always said he didn't mind a horse as long as it was someone else's, and he wasn't taking care of the horse. Dad's dislike for horses could really be seen whenever he was around Toby. Toby had eventually become a one-man horse, since I was the only person in my family ever to do anything with him. On occasion,

Dad would go into Toby's pen, and the horse would immediately lay his ears back, whirl about, and pretend he was going to kick. This, of course, would send my father sprawling over the fence in retreat. I always had to chuckle inwardly at how Toby could bluff my father. I knew he was bluffing, because Toby didn't have a mean bone in his body and wouldn't ever have kicked anyone.

At any rate, I finally talked Dad into riding Dixie in the trail ride with Toby and me. Once at the event, both horses acted exceptionally well throughout the entire day. It was thrilling for me to have Dad by my side as we meandered through the sweet-smelling forest and crossed the bubbling streams. One can get so much closer to the beauty and solitude of nature while on horseback. When the day was over, Dad commented how he had really enjoyed the day, even if it had been with a bunch of horses.

It seems ironic to me that my father could dislike and mistrust horses so much, and I could feel so totally the opposite. Unfortunately, however, there were times when I trusted horses too much.

As I have already explained, Dixie had been my pet almost from the day she was foaled. Each day of her life, I had fed her, played with her, and cared for her. I had trained Dixie to do tricks, ride, and come on command (with a whistle). Never did it enter my mind that she, like any other horse, had powerful kicking legs.

Dixie had scraped her hind leg on a rock while I had been riding her. The scrape was just above her rear hoof. I called Dad over to help me so I could treat the wound. Dad held onto Dixie's halter, and I proceeded to spray the wound dressing onto the sore from an aerosol can. Without thinking how powerful my horse was or imagining my friendly animal's ability to "plaster" me, I kneeled down. With my face only a slight distance away from her rear leg, I sprayed the hand-held can. Apparently it created a stinging sensation in her leg, because the next detail I remember was getting picked up from the ground by my father. With blood utterly squirting from my nose, Dad told me what had happened. Evidently, Dixie had kicked me squarely in the middle of the face. The impact broke my eyeglasses right down the middle. The thrust of Dixie's kick sent me flying backward several feet. Later, an x-ray at the hospital revealed my nose had been cracked by the ordeal. Dad went on for days about how lucky I had been not to have had my head kicked in and been killed. He kept repeating that he hoped Dixie had knocked some sense into me, so I wouldn't ever do such a foolish trick again.

The summer after graduating from high school, I began a new project with Toby. It all started when I went to visit an old horse trader named Mert. Mert was a kind old man who loved horses more than anything. I often spent many hours just talking with him about either horse equipment or horses. On one occasion, I stopped at Mert's place, and he said he had a surprise to show me. I anxiously followed him to his shed, and there before me was a beautiful, antique, single-horse buggy. Mert figured the buggy to be about eighty years old. I immediately fell in love with the antique and asked if I could buy it. Mert said he'd kind of figured I might buy the buggy, so he quoted me a fair price and I happily paid him. I also bought a finely crafted, Amish, handmade, leather harness. With all the parts for a new horse project, I set out for home to begin.

Bob was a neighbor who always had horses on his farm. Several of them could drive. I asked Bob one day if he'd help me train Toby to pull the buggy, since I had no idea how to begin. Bob said he'd be more than happy to assist me. Since I was from a generation removed from the olden days of farming with horses, I didn't even know how to put the complicated harness on Toby. With Bob's help, Toby was soon getting use to his new harness. The first step was to put on the harness. Next Bob would pretend to drive Toby from the rear, while I slowly led him from his head. Toby couldn't figure out how someone could steer him about without sitting on his back. When Toby could finally be driven all over the farm with someone walking and handling the harness reins from the back, we hooked up the buggy. My day was made when that beautiful horse, attached to the buggy, went striding down the road for all to see.

Toby and I were soon the talk of many of our neighbors and townspeople as we proudly drove around the countryside. Few, if any, youths of my generation have ever had the desire to travel by such primitive means of transportation as a horse and buggy.

All was going well that summer until total disaster broke loose. One warm summer evening, Toby had driven me around the countryside. Upon returning to the farm, I drove Toby to my tack room to unhitch the buggy and harness. The disastrous mistake I made that evening was not immediately unhooking the buggy from Toby. Bob had always stressed that, should a horse get spooked, so long as the buggy is unhooked and put out of the way, no damage can result. Toby was suddenly startled and his large frame proved to be too much stress for the eighty year-old wood on the buggy, and the wooden pole to which the horse was attached to the buggy snapped. The loud snap caused my horse to get further unsettled, and the next detail I remember was the sharp, freshly broken edge of the pole impaling Toby's rear thigh. The pole, like a sharp dagger, plunged through his leg muscle and came out the other side. At this point, I knew nothing could prevent what was about to happen. Toby went crazy with pain and took off at a dead run with the harness and buggy still attached. I went screaming after him as I watched my lovely buggy roll over and over and over. Toby finally went blindly crashing, head first, into a steel cattle gate, which all but knocked him unconscious. At this point, he was dazed enough so I was able to catch up to him and settle him down enough to lead him back to his pen. I assure you, I didn't have to unharness him or unhook the buggy, because, when the ordeal was over, he had left bits and pieces of them strewn all over the farm.

With blood streaming from Toby's leg, I summoned a veterinarian. The vet looked over the wound, treated it, and stitched it shut. Dr. Larson told me how lucky I'd been that Toby had missed severing the main artery in his leg. The wound had missed the artery by about a half-inch. Had the edge of the pole cut through the artery, the horse would have died from blood loss before the vet could have reached the farm.

After this unfortunate encounter, I set out to piece my prized buggy and harness back together again. For weeks I hammered, sawed, and painted my buggy. Mert had sent the harness and parts of the buggy back to some Amish people he knew. Their fine craftsmen would be able to do a fine repair job, Mert had assured me.

In time, my harness and buggy were as good as before, and even Toby miraculously healed up without even a scar on his leg. Thankfully, I had everything work out for the best, but I had certainly learned a lesson the hard way.

Dixie's turn came, one day, to be in the limelight. I always felt both horses were special to me, but Dixie often had a hard time competing with Toby. Dixie was in season, and I decided I'd like to try raising another foal. After giving the idea some consideration, I chose a mule as the kind of foal I wanted.

My entire life I've never been accused of being too conventional, and once again this move proved it. I had lots of friends and neighbors with ponies and horses, but none had a mule. I could envision nothing more unique than riding a mule down the road some day. In order to produce a mule foal from a horse mare, one must cross the mare with a jackass. I knew of one in a neighboring county and proceeded to take Dixie to be bred. When the mating had taken place, Dixie and I returned home for the standard eleven-month wait.

The following year, Dixie became a mother for the first time. While checking the pasture one day, to my delight, a newborn, sorrel-colored, long-eared mule foal was by Dixie's side. I was as proud of the newcomer as Dixie was. Snuff was the name I chose for the little mule as a joke aimed at my father, who has always loved chewing tobacco, or snuff, as it is sometimes called. The other reason for the name was that the youngster was the same color as snuff. For three days I watched and played with Snuff. He was a dream come true to me.

On the third day, however, I learned another traumatic lesson about God's will in relation to life and death.

As I walked up to little Snuff lying in the grass next to Dixie, I was so pleased at his cuteness and individuality.

Already I was forming a true love for the little, odd-looking creature. I patted Snuff on the rump so he would stand up, but he just lay there. Once again I thumped him, but to no avail. To my horror, I realized he was almost dead. I ran for the house, pulled Jerry and Julie out, hopped in the pickup truck, and steamed for the pasture. I carefully loaded my small foal in the back with Julie and Jerry holding him. I then took off for town in hope of finding the veterinarian at his office. I was so upset I could hardly drive straight, as I raced well above the speed limit toward town. Luckily the vet was just preparing to venture out on another call when we arrived. He examined the mule colt and said it didn't look as if the chances were good.

"What's the matter with him, Doc?" I cried.

"I'd say the mother hasn't let him nurse since he's been born, and now he's about dead from starvation and dehydration," replied the vet.

"But I saw him at her back end all the time," I returned.

"That's just the point. The mare was either not letting her milk down or else never letting him get a good drink of milk. Finally, by the third day, it was about all but over for this little fellow," commented the vet.

The vet gave Snuff some drugs intravenously and pumped fluids into his system. He informed me that all I could do then was wait and keep the colt cool.

Once again we headed for home. I carried Snuff into the old barn so he was out of the blistering sun. My little friend was in a comatose state and was laboriously trying to continue the breathing process. I quickly ran to the pasture, grabbed Dixie, and looked underneath her. Sure enough, she showed no signs of ever having nursed her foal. I almost dropped at the thought of my mule dying, simply because I had been too negligent to notice he hadn't been nursing. I knew I couldn't blame Dixie, because new mares often are ticklish in the back and won't nurse their offspring without some assistance.

I returned to the barn and lay Snuff's weak, tiny head upon my lap. For two long hours I cupped his head in my hands and prayed for his life. Suddenly his breathing became staggered; first with a breath, a long pause, and then another breath. Before long, the breaths came no more. I sat there in total disbelief. How could this have happened? One moment Snuff was frolicking and full of life, and the next moment, still. I often wonder if we are ever too old to cry or show our hurt emotions. Here I was, nineteen years old, crying again, just as I had when my little puppy was killed years ago.

Without informing anyone in my family, I carried my dead foal to a shady evergreen tree, dug a hole in the ground, and laid Snuff to eternal rest. So many times since that day I have relived that emotional scene and pondered on ways I could have prevented the final outcome.

Time was rolling forward, as was always the case. In the fall, I was to begin college at the University of Minnesota. A crucial decision faced me. Not only did I need additional money for my schooling, but Dad had already informed me he was not caring for my horses the entire time I was off at school. Once again I knew I would have to part with my beloved friends. Why is an animal so easy to adopt and love, yet always so hard to part with? I advertised Dixie, Toby, and all my equipment in the paper, much as I had when I'd owned my ponies.

Within days, the buggy, harness, Dixie, and Toby were gone from the farm. I sadly waved as they left in a cloud of dust down the gravel road. I knew I'd probably never see Dixie again, but I had made an oral agreement with the new owner of Toby. The agreement stated that, in a few years, after I had graduated from college, if everyone involved wanted, I could buy Toby back again. Just having that knowledge gave me great peace of mind as I left for school that fall.

Four years later, I returned home to go into a farming partnership with my father and brother. Shortly after returning home, I called the man who had purchased Toby.

"Roger, do you still want to sell Toby back to me?" I questioned with anticipation.

"That horse was the best I've ever owned, Scott, but yes, I was planning on honoring our agreement," replied Roger.

"What seems to be the problem then?" I asked.

"Last week we had a bad thunderstorm here, and Toby was out in the pasture. I hate to tell you this, but he was struck by lightning and killed."

Silence . . . .

"I'm sorry to hear that," I said at last as the tears began welling up in my eyes.

"Goodbye," I uttered as I replaced the phone on the hook as though in slow motion.

The process goes on and on. Great animals come and go, just as we human beings come and go. I still envision Toby up in the sky somewhere, running like the endless wind and never giving in to defeat.

My horse friends have provided many fond memories as well as heartbreaking ones. I can never recapture my moments with those horses, but never will I forget them or stop loving them, either.

11

○ ○ ○ ○

The Night Fire

In a previous chapter I outlined my family's poultry operation. The work involved with caring for thousands of hens is immense, to say the least. The burden of that farming enterprise most certainly put a huge strain on all my family members. Odd as it may seem, I learned to dislike eggs so greatly as a youngster gathering them that, even as an adult, I can't eat eggs. The chicken operation definitely laid the groundwork for my psychological feelings that remained later in life. Once, while I was participating in high school sports, my coach had our team eat eggs for breakfast at an away game. I tried arguing with him, but he insisted eggs were the best food for us, and everyone would eat the same. For the rest of that day, I performed terribly, because of my horrible stomach pains from eating eggs for breakfast.

Not only did my family have a chicken operation back in those years, but, coincidentally, so did our next door neighbors. Bob and Marge were good friends with my folks. They were approximately the same age as my parents, and their children were about the same age as my siblings and I. Many countless hours were spent by all members of both families working or playing together. Dad and Bob would often help each other with field work. My mother and Marge spent many moments together discussing everything imaginable. Reese and Dale were close to my age and Jerry's, so one can imagine the fun we could strum up. The four of us were always exploring by the creek or investigating the large woods at the extreme rear of our farm.

The neighbor's chicken system was larger than our own. In their single, massive, loose-housing barn, one could see eight thousand hens moving about. With imagination, one could picture the inside as a monstrous, living snowstorm.

Bob's facilities were immaculate. Not only was his business large, but it was well kept up. One could always see the twinkle of pride in his eyes, as he happily showed people the operation.

One night, as I lay in bed asleep, something brought me from the shrouds of somnolence. For some freakish reason, my upstairs bedroom contained an orange glow. I was positive I'd just had a terrible nightmare, but, in reality, the nightmare had only begun.

For a moment I lay there in fear. The strange glow seemed to flicker occasionally, which sent shivers within my body. At first I thought I had died, or was about to, and perhaps one got to view hell, before getting whisked off to heaven. Suddenly I came to my senses. The alarm clock next to my bed showed two A.M. on its face. I leaped out of bed and ran to the window. To my astonishment the orange glow was all over our farm. The source of this glow, however, escaped me. From my two-story-height advantage, where my bedroom was located, I could see everything on our farm. I carefully checked each building, but saw nothing. Then it dawned on me. Perhaps a comet was heading straight for earth! I peered into the sky but could find nothing except small, twinkling stars on a black background.

Unwilling to halt my search, I proceeded to tiptoe into Julie's room, which was adjacent to mine, and see what was on her side of the house. I quickly found the source of the flickering glow.

Across the road from our farm, Bob and Marge's huge chicken barn was burning. In a flash I was back in my room pulling on my clothes and screaming for my father in the lower half of the house.

By the time I made it downstairs, Dad was already dressed and on the phone.

"Hello, fire department. Bob's chicken house is on fire, so get right out here!" my father directed.

Dad hung up the receiver and quickly exited the house with me on his heels. As we ran across the road and into Bob's yard, I remember thinking how strange the familiar sights looked under the existing circumstances. The enticing creek seemed awesome and terrifying. The pasture I loved to romp in seemed so haunted looking.

My father and I began knocking on Bob and Marge's door. I didn't think they would ever wake up, but, before long, Bob was awake, dressed, and running for the all-consuming blaze. As Dad and Bob sped for the barn, I remember Bob's uttering over and over "Oh, my God, oh, my God."

The blaze, until that moment, had been contained mostly in the front section of the upstairs. Dad and Bob were hoping to open some door quickly and then possibly start moving some of the expensive egg-handling equipment out of the barn. Suddenly, the shingles of the large building caught on fire, and then, as though fed by dynamite, the engulfing blaze exploded across the entire roof.

My father and Bob halted in their tracks as the intense heat kept them at a distance. With the sound of sirens in the distance, my dad and Bob agreed the most important problem was now to keep the surrounding buildings from burning.

My mother had come over, and I could see her comforting Marge on the front steps of the house. The future of Bob and Marge's poultry setup looked dismal. We all just stared blindly at the fire.

Into the yard came two speeding fire trucks and a water tank truck. To my unbelieving eyes, there came car after car behind the fire department. I could understand people going to see a fire, but I wouldn't have believed this many people coming out at two in the morning. Within minutes, the entire yard was jammed with vehicles and people.

The firemen dispatched their duties with swiftness and professionalism. Such a fine service these brave men provide in harsh moments! There was little doubt by this time: The barn didn't have a chance. The firemen aimed their several hoses at the surrounding buildings to stop the chances of their burning, too. It was then I noticed how the extreme heat had blistered the paint completely off the walls of the other buildings. As the cool water hit the surface of the buildings, huge jets of steam hissed up into the eerie sky. Before long, the hot wood certainly might have caught fire.

With all the action and incredible sights, it was easy to forget one important consideration. Inside that barn, was the largest, living chicken roast to probably ever take place. I began thinking about this at the same moment as the putrid odor of eight thousand incinerating chickens struck my nostrils. One can't imagine how sickening the smell of all those burning feathers could be.

As could be expected, after the shingles of the roof were burned, the rafters caught fire next. But now the intensely blazing roof was falling in. The horrible detail was that not only were chickens on the inside bedded with wood shaving, but the building itself was constructed almost exclusively of wood. Once the roof began falling to the wood-shaving-bedded floor, the inside of the barn began looking like purgatory.

Bob watched through the entire ordeal in silent shock and disbelief. His marvelous structure was now mere rubble. All his hopes and dreams were burning up with his building. Marge, Reese, and Dale watched with tears in their eyes as the immense barn was razed.

The firemen speculated that the fire was caused by faulty wiring, since the first blaze had been spotted by Dad and me in the corner of the roof. It was in this corner that the main power line fed the barn with electricity. Ironically, the electricity had also fed doom into the barn.

By and by, the awesome orange glow grew dimmer and dimmer. Eventually, the intense heat started fading, and the nauseating smell from within the barn subsided. Before long, one car after another made its way out the driveway and on down the road for home.

I sat there watching and thinking. To me, it seemed as though Dad and I had just aroused Bob from bed, and now, in what seemed only moments later, the fire was nearly over, the people and the fire trucks gone, and only my family and Bob's remained.

Finally, Dad comforted Bob one last time by patting him on the back and offering our assistance in the morning. My mother hugged Marge and told her it would be all right. I said good night to my friends Reese and Dale, and we walked back across the road to our farm. I assure you, however, I really don't think any member of either family really slept a wink for the remainder of that night.

Bright and early the following day, Dad and I were at Bob's place as promised. We peered through the still-smoldering rubble for anything salvageable. Try as we could, though, nothing could be found. The intense heat had either burned or melted everything in its path.

As I looked out across the pasture, I noticed a peculiar sight. Scattered about were a few hens. Reese and I headed in their direction for a closer analysis. Along the way, we found several dead or dying hens with badly charred bodies and feathers. To our unbelieving eyes, though, eight hens had somehow survived the fire. I distinctly remember envisioning the poem "The Charge of the Light Brigade." Into the valley of death rode the six hundred and only six rode out again. This time, eight thousand birds had ridden in, and eight ridden out. A couple of the hens looked rather delirious. Apparently, they had suffered some brain damage, because they kept walking in circles and staring blindly ahead. The other hens, however, happily scratched about, looking for food and not really caring about anyone or anything.

Reese and I ran back to our fathers to find out how the few hens could have escaped their death chamber. Both Dad and Bob felt the hens had probably flown to safety just after the roof had collapsed. By some small chance, the survivors had flown straight up and out of the barn where the roof had been.

This explained all the dead hens outside. Perhaps they too had tried escaping, but possibly the hens had caught on fire and like a living torch, had plummeted to their deaths.

Reese and I continued our exploration. Inside the still-hot walls of the barn was a charred mass of rubble. I still remember getting rather queasy as I looked at the thousands of almost-indistinguishable hen carcasses lying about the floor.

The barn actually smoldered and smoked for over a week after the blaze. Finally, after a quenching rain one day, the last drift of smoke subsided.

In a few days a huge bulldozer had found its way onto our neighbor's farm. I watched in amazement as the powerful, steel-tracked machine dug an immense hole. Upon completion of the hole, the dozer, bit by bit, pushed the remains of the barn into the cavity. Finally, the ground was bare where the barn had been, and the bulldozer covered up the hole.

Bob and Marge informed my family one day they were moving away. This came as a tremendous surprise. To this day, I often wonder why they decided to relocate. Perhaps the fire had posed too much of a hardship on them, or maybe they wanted a change of scenery in hope of losing the memory of that awful night.

Bob, Marge, Reese, and Dale all moved to somewhere in northern Minnesota. For a while, my family corresponded with them. In time, though, we lost touch with each other and never wrote again.

As I grew older, I would think back from time to time about that spooky night. As was always the case with the folk and their fauna, animals come and go, loved ones come and go, and good neighbors come and go. This time, many lives had been forever altered by the night fire.

12

○ ○ ○ ○

Here, Kitty, Kitty

Although cats have never been as popular with me as perhaps my horses or dogs, I have had some interesting times with various cats.

Long ago, in the early days of my life, I described Mother Cat. She was a fine representative of the grimalkin population.

Many years later, another interesting feline showed up in the picture. One of our female farm cats had given birth to a litter of cute, cuddly, furry kittens. As with any set of new kittens, my brother, sister, and I would almost kill them with affection. In the litter of multicolored kittens was definitely a special youngster.

"Boots" was the outsider from the start of his existence. He was yellow in color with four white paws, which is why my sister named the kitten Boots. He was larger, wilder, and rougher than any of his littermates. From the time his little eyes first opened, he could beat any of his siblings in a fight. Try as we could, Jerry, Julie, and I couldn't tame the "oddball" kitten. In time, Boots strayed from the farm, and my family, eventually, assumed he had been killed.

Many months later, I spotted a huge yellow cat stalking through the grass of our pasture. I ran out to investigate, and, to my surprise, the cat took off running on four white paws. My family realized after that incident, Boots had not perished but was actually "living off the land," one might say.

Only occasionally did any member of my family chance to see the large tomcat. When Boots was spotted, it was often miles from the farm. Boots must have felt a tremendous "call of the wild," because he actually acted like a wild animal. Without a doubt, this cat was self-sufficient. I had periodically checked with neighboring farmers, and they always informed me they hadn't ever fed the big cat. The only time they ever saw him was when one of their own female cats came in season. Old Boots would then come slithering into their farm, do his male duties, and then take off again. Word had it that Boots was seldom challenged by another tomcat, which was also unusual when it came to mating cats.

Many years passed by, and we began forgetting about Boots. Now that I think back, however, it does seem odd how many of our farm cats kept having litters of yellow kittens. Many times these kittens had one or several white paws.

The most surprising occurrence I remember came about a decade after Boots was born. No one had seen the huge tomcat for years, and this time he was definitely assumed dead.

I returned home one fine winter weekend from college. Jerry and I had decided to do a little rabbit hunting in the woods beyond our farm. After a long, laborious trek through the deep snow, we came to the edge of the trees. With a brief pause to regain our breath, we went into the woods to begin our hunt. We eventually stopped to rest after pushing through the dense trees, underbrush, and snow. Jerry and I started laughing at how red faced and out of breath we were. As I looked upward, I remember commenting on how thick the woods were. At that point my eyes almost fell out, and my heart just about stopped. High in the branches of a big oak tree was perched a cat. Not just any cat, but a monstrous yellow one with glaring, piercing eyes. The sight of it almost sent shivers down my spine. The cat seemed like a lion or tiger ready to attack us trespassers.

Jerry suddenly broke the silence and shouted, "Hey, its Boots. Man, is he big!"

I certainly couldn't argue that point. Sure enough, though, this feline was the long-forgotten Boots. Later that day, upon returning to the farm, Jerry and I informed everyone of our discovery.

Once again, it's been years since Boots has been seen, but those yellow kittens keep popping up on the farm. I never know even today if the kittens are genetic carryovers or if the big cat still roams the wild.

About the time Jerry was eight, Julie was ten, and I was twelve, my mother let us in on a surprise. Our quaint little five-member family was going to become six, because mother was pregnant. We were all more than overjoyed, but I remember thinking how it was getting rather late to start a family again.

Mom went throughout her pregnancy working hard on the farm. She did, in fact, leave from doing chores to go to the hospital on the day of the birth of her fourth child.

Sally was born on a fine September fall day. When Dad and Mom brought the pretty, blond-haired, blue-eyed baby home, our family was full of joyful bliss. To this day I'm thankful Mom had another baby, because I learned to appreciate children much more.

To our total astonishment, Mom informed us one day Dad and she had decided it would be hard on Sally to grow up without another brother or sister her own age to play with. Mom said she was pregnant again. About then I started thinking, *One baby is fine, but two bawling, runny-nosed, poopy-diapered babies is getting too extreme.* There wasn't much that could be done by this time, and, eighteen months after Sally's birth, Marcia came on the scene.

Of *all the luck,* I thought. Now, instead of one sister, I had three. Jerry and I had quickly become outnumbered. Julie was already starting to get on my nerves, because I couldn't even breathe or she would tattle on me to Mom. I figured with three sisters, I'd surely be doomed.

Sally and Marcia were picture-perfect sisters. I was glad they were born when I was old enough to understand and appreciate them. From the beginning, they played together and amused each other. It was after the two girls were old enough to talk that we really started getting laughs about their antics with cats.

Sally would choose several cats for herself, and Marcia, the others for her own. The names they created were invariably classics. The first cat Sally ever named was a fluffy-haired, gray cat. When Sally was quite small, she had once reached to grab the cat. As young children often do, Sally squeezed the poor cat. In defense, it scratched Sally. My family still chuckles when we remember how Sally came running to the house in tears and mumbling how the naughty kitty had hurt her. For the entire life of that cat, Naughty Kitty was its name.

Marcia similarly had humorous names for cats. While Marcia was in her early schooldays, she had a teacher she didn't care for, called Mrs. Gillman. Marcia was always spouting off about how Mrs. Gillman was ornery. It happened that one of Marcia's cats reminded her of this teacher. Sure enough, Gillman became the christened name of the cat.

My two little sisters had their bad moments also. They enjoyed life on the farm tremendously and loved the animals they were around. Unfortunately, as with all beloved animals, occasionally one gets hurt or dies. Whenever such an incident occurred, Sally and Marcia always shed many sorrowful tears.

One of the favorite farm cats was a big overweight, lovable tomcat called Toma. Toma was a direct descendent of Boots, except, instead of being yellow, he was gray with white paws. Actually Toma was a cross between Marcia's gray-colored Gillman female cat and the infamous Boots.

Toma was the head male cat for many years on our farm. It was always so comical to see the fat tomcat come waddling toward someone. His actions were at all times the same. If he spotted a person with the potential to administer attention, he would head toward the person. Whenever Toma was within five feet, he would lie down, roll over, rub his back on the ground with his feet straight in the air, then sit up and meow. Normally, by the time all those actions had taken place, the person couldn't help but give Toma some attention.

Toma really got himself into trouble one day. On a cold fall day just prior to winter, my father and I decided to run to town in our pickup truck and buy some supplies. As most everyone knows, cats love to lie wherever it is warm, especially on a cold day. Just shortly before our trip to town, Mom had driven the pickup truck to run an errand,. Unknown to Dad or me, Toma had decided the warm engine of the truck was the place to be on such a blustery day. He evidently climbed in from underneath the truck's engine and stationed himself in a most comfortable position underneath the hood. Dad and I came out of the house, got into the truck, started the engine, and off we drove. As we casually chatted back and forth in the cab, Toma was going through torture. When at last we were at our destination, we hopped out and started walking from the pickup truck. At that point we heard the most back-tingling yowling one could possibly imagine coming from under the hood. I let Dad buy the supplies while I calmed Toma in the cab of the truck. Old Toma never went near another vehicle after that incident.

When my little sisters were a little older, another interesting cat came on the scene. Marcia and Sally were about eight and nine years old by this time. They grabbed Jerry and me one day to show us something terrible. One of the female cats had given birth to a litter of kittens. Unfortunately, we were experiencing some miserable January weather in Minnesota, and all the kittens but one had frozen to death. As you might well imagine, the girls adopted the pathetic little creature and set out to see that he survived. The kitten was moved into the warm dairy barn and given almost limitless attention by everyone in my family. Marcia really learned to love this kitten. As time passed, we began noticing something peculiar about the kitten. Its ears were getting smaller and smaller. Dad finally figured out what had happened. The same killing cold that had extinguished this kitten's brothers and sisters most likely had frozen his ears. The dead tissue was simply falling off. Eventually the kitten lost almost his entire ears. I must admit it posed a comical picture. The cat soon became known as Ears Kitty, even though Marcia thought the name was cruel and insisted on Puff for a name. Jerry and I often clowned around and would call the cat in the same manner we called the other cats. The difference, though, was instead of "Here, kitty, kitty," we called, "Ears, kitty, kitty."

Ears Kitty not only outlived the killing cold that year but also many diseases, like distemper and pneumonia. No matter what the odds, this cat seemed to persevere and went on to live a long, full life. Ears Kitty played yet another role in our farm's continuous rotation of animal life.

A few years later, while attending the University of Minnesota in St. Paul, I developed yet another interesting relationship with a cat.

I was working toward a double Bachelor of Science Degree in Animal Science and Agriculture Education. Attaining a college education is quite expensive, so I decided to work my way through school at the university's research dairy barn. I had chosen to do this soon after moving to the city. It had only taken me about two days to realize I couldn't stand not being around animals. To make my situation all the worse, this was the first time in my life where I was forced to be from the farm four or five years. I worked in the research dairy barn for approximately four years, and, to this day, I still maintain it's the only reason I stayed sane throughout my schooling. Don't think it was easy, however. During my entire college career, I worked an average of about forty hours per week, while carrying a full, sixteen-credit school load besides. The only way this could be accomplished, though, was to start milking at three o'clock in the morning, work until about eleven o'clock and then scurry off to classes all day. Unfortunately, many a professor went unheard by me, as I would often drift off to sleep from exhaustion. Due to my constant need for money, I worked almost all the weekends and holidays. I was occasionally a little bothered at how many of my friends would leave the big city and take off for their homes each weekend, while I had to keep up the "grind." To my total dismay, I was seldom ever able to return to my family farm more than once every six or eight weeks. When I did finally graduate, however, I did so with a true sense of accomplishment, because I had totally worked my way through college without any help from my parents.

It was in the dairy research barn I came across that cat that is the subject of my next tale. The barn was just like any other barn on any farm in the country. Within its holds were one hundred cows, many calves, bulls, mice, and cats. I really enjoyed my work in the barn, because, while there, I could forget all about an upcoming exam or some other form of pressure and just dairy farm. I used to think I was pretty smart when I'd return to my apartment surrounded by all my city neighbors and have manure on my pants.

The barn had cats like any other barn. As I already stated, wherever there is grain, there are usually mice. For this reason, the cats, mice, and cows went hand in hand within the U of M dairy barn. I enjoyed taking some fresh, warm milk I'd recently taken from a cow and pouring it into the cat dish. All the cats would meow with pure delight.

I remember one occasion when some new kittens were born. Shortly after the furry kittens came into existence, the barn cats came down with a fatal disease called distemper. Once a cat or dog contracts the disease, little can be done to save its life. Dogs are generally vaccinated to prevent distemper, but cats are usually bypassed because they are too numerous on most farms to justify the expense of the vaccine. One by one, the cats started disappearing. Cats, like many animals, when sick or dying seek out a secluded place. For this reason, one seldom finds a dead cat lying around. As could be expected, the new kitten also started coughing and showing the dreaded symptoms of distemper. One of my dairy-barn coworkers, whose name was Brian, decided to try to help the kittens. Brian was studying to be a veterinarian, so he knew the odds were not good for the kittens to survive. He used his own money to have the university veterinarians try to cure the kittens. In several weeks, Brian returned to the barn with a somewhat-healthy-looking cat in his arms.

"Hey, Scott, this is the only survivor out of all those kittens I took in," Brian told me.

"One survivor is better than none, Brian," I replied.

The young gray-and-white cat was added to the severely depleted supply of barn cats. I couldn't believe how few cats remained. Only a few weeks earlier, there had been about fifteen cats roaming throughout the barn. Now, after the disease had taken its toll, only four felines remained.

The next series of events led to my eventual acquisition of the gray-and-white cat. Just as the cat population had dwindled, so too had the mouse population. It is a well-known fact that cats can't survive on solely a milk diet. They must have some form of protein in addition. With the mouse supply low, the cats began looking terribly gaunt and hungry. Once again, Brian's compassion for animals showed through, as he used his own money to purchase cat food. The cat food, however, was too little and too infrequent to keep the cats really healthy.

About that time, the young gray-and-white cat started showing some exceptionally intelligent signs.

After our first series of morning chores were done in the barn, all of us students would sit around for a short break and eat some sandwiches or cookies. The gray-and white cat would hop up in someone's lap and with tremendous enthusiasm start licking that person's face. Without fail, this peculiar action always netted him a bite of cookie or sandwich. Never had I seen a cat with the same lapping characteristics as a dog. Even when one poked a teasing finger toward the cat's face, he quickly had his small, flicking tongue on it. Before long, the cat was nicknamed "Lick."

Lick was such a friendly little fellow; I soon began taking a real liking to him. It amazed me how he had been smart enough to discover an innovative way of survival. The few handouts, though, didn't provide enough nutrition for the poor fellow ever to look anything but thin and scrawny.

For several days I kept reviewing a plan I'd been mustering up. I knew no one at the barn would care if Lick was removed and taken to a good home. Seeing those poor cats dying off was surely not a pleasant sight to view. My problem was with my apartment. I wanted so badly to bring Lick home so I could have a warm, friendly cat to buddy with on the lonely nights while I studied. The dilemma was my apartment had a "no-pets-allowed" ruling. This ruling kept bothering me, because I knew of at least two other apartment dwellers who had been evicted because of either being caught with a pet or having pet damage within their apartments.

At last I decided to make an attempt with Lick despite the possible complications. I first made all the necessary preparations within my apartment. I purchased a litter pan, cat food, cat dish, and some toys with bells on them. Next I drove to the campus dairy barn, put Lick in a burlap sack (which he thoroughly hated), loaded him into my pickup truck, and returned to my apartment. I then cautiously carried the sack and its contents into my apartment and shut the door.

The real fun began soon after I acquired Lick. I was feeling like a felon because of my cat. Everyone thought I was suddenly antisocial, because, at all times, I kept my curtains drawn. Even on nice, sunny days, I kept the apartment closed to outside viewers for obvious reasons. My next series of problems involved many severe reprimanding of Lick, when he either meowed or tried scratching on the walls or furniture. Lick actually started getting mad at me, because I would scold and spank him every time he'd open his mouth. I knew I'd be in a lot of trouble, though, if a passing neighbor ever heard a meow from behind my door. The other difficult task was to try secretly to smuggle cat food in and smuggle out cat litter. On several other occasions, neighbors would knock on my door, wanting to come in and visit. Upon hearing any knock, I would grab Lick, throw him in a closet, shut the door, and then let the person in. The entire time anyone was in my apartment, I would be fidgety and nervous. All I could ever think about was that if Lick started meowing, then we'd both get kicked out in the street. Lick, however, was normally rather good, and in the two years he and I were together, we were never discovered. I did feel bad that Lick couldn't ever go outside, but then I figured, if given the chance to choose, he would have chosen this anyway. After all, he surely would have perished at the barn. Now he was fat, sassy, and healthy. I also made sure he got all his vaccinations.

Lick and I went through some good and some bad times. I loved having him as a pet. During my college days, I got to be quite a homebody. I envied my buddies who went to school by day and parties by night. With my job, school, and studies, however, I was usually so exhausted that all I ever had strength left to do was return to my apartment. When at my apartment, I would lie on the sofa, turn on the television set, and relax for a while. Lick would generally hop up on my stomach, lick my arm, cuddle up in a ball, and go happily to sleep. Times like those made the problem of owning Lick more worthwhile.

The bad times are rather comical to remember also, as I think back. One incident I remember vividly happened soon after I brought Lick home. For several weeks, Lick detested the sight of me. If I wasn't spanking him for jumping on the sofa and looking out the window, I was yelling at him for meowing. It got to the point when, as soon as I'd walk through my apartment door, Lick would lay his ears back and run off to the other room.

On one particular occasion, I had fallen asleep on the sofa while studying. All of a sudden, Lick jumped up on my legs and bit me right in the knee. I'm still unsure of whether his act was in violence or in fun, but nonetheless, it brought me painfully out of my slumbering state. I remember yelling, grabbing Lick around his middle, and throwing him as hard as I could. The cat went flying through the air completely across my living room. Lick then went smacking into the wall high in the air where the ceiling and closet door met. When he finally landed on the ground, he sped off and pouted for hours.

Another problem I was burdened with was my water bed. One can imagine what a cat's claws could do to a water bed. As one might expect, Lick's favorite place to sneak was my bed. All Lick could see was a warm, soft, comfortable place to sleep. All I could see were potential holes spouting water all about. I disciplined Lick at every opportunity on this matter. Eventually, Lick understood all his boundaries and was seldom a problem. For a while, though, I didn't think I would survive the ordeal.

In the two years Lick and I were together, he grew immensely. His appetite was definitely nothing short of a lion's. My friends laughed at me when I told them I had to buy cat food in fifty-pound sacks. Lick loved eating so much; he kept getting fatter and fatter, even though I tried rationing his food. The term "finicky as a cat" surely wasn't ever meant to describe my cat. By the time Lick and I parted, he had gone from a scrawny, hungry cat to an immense, thirteen-pound monster. Not only had my cat-food bills increased significantly, but my trips to empty out the litter box also increased.

The time finally came when I graduated from college and moved from the city. Lick and I had become quite good friends, but I wasn't sure what to do with him then. If brought back to the U of M dairy barn, he'd run the same risk as before. I knew taking him home to my family's farm wasn't a good idea, because my folks didn't want a house cat. With all his pampering over the past couple years, Lick probably wouldn't have fared well with the outside elements on our farm, either.

At last a girl I knew quite well while attending school decided she'd like Lick as a pet in her apartment. I was happy Lick had found a good home, because it made leaving him and my home in the city much easier.

My final yarn about cats takes place on my own farm. I've always enjoyed a cat with something a bit peculiar about it. It was for this reason Ears Kitty was so popular with me. His lack of ears definitely made him more of a peculiarity. On my farm I have approximately a dozen cats in all sizes, colors, and shapes. Two old female cats, in particular, are my favorites.

The younger of the two is a solid-black feline, whose age is about ten years old. The female cat's name is Musta Black (Musta being the Finnish word for black). The other cat is a multicolored calico, who is about fourteen. This old girl's title is Wilma. Now what makes Musta Black and Wilma so unique, one might ask? To begin with, they both have rather severe handicaps.

Everyone knows the importance of sound legs for a cat. A cat puts a lot of dependence on his running, grabbing, and clawing ability. Musta Black was injured years ago when a cow stepped on her front leg and broke it. When the leg healed, it did so in such a fashion that it cannot be used. The leg is twisted inward and locked in a bent position.

Old Musta Black just hobbles around on three legs, because she couldn't use her front leg even if she tried.

Wilma is a classic, because she has hardly any teeth. Just as a cat's legs are essential for survival, so are his teeth for killing, eating, and so forth. Old Wilma has only one canine tooth on the top of her mouth and a couple of teeth left on the bottom.

At this point one might think, "Oh, the poor cats. They must be miserable."

This is exactly what I used to think. With time and observation, however, I soon learned how wrong my assumptions had been. I doubt if there are cats anywhere that have the mousing ability of these two old felines. Impaired as they are, they form a team unparalleled by any.

I've seen the two of them pair up, climb trees, and capture birds right out of the tree. They also work well together when trying to capture a rodent. How they do it, I'll never know, but I've even seen Wilma and Musta Black drag squirrels and rabbits into my barn for their kittens to feed upon.

I invariably start laughing every time I see old Wilma come proudly strutting into the barn with some limp, lifeless bird or mouse hanging in her mouth. I never have had any idea how she actually kills a mouse or bird. Most of the time I reach down to pet Wilma as she struts by, then laughingly tell her she gummed another one to death. The amazing factor is that Wilma can never eat her own catch. She actually loves to hunt just for the sake of it, but she continually turns the catch over to the other cats in the barn. Without teeth, she can't devour much of what she catches.

Musta Black and Wilma draw a chuckle out of me almost every day, as I watch them going about their normal routines. They have given me many years of enjoyment, and I hope they are around for years to come.

Undoubtedly, since I am a farmer, my cat stories are far from ended. With each passing year, some old cats die, and some new kittens are born. As I look at the cats in my barn, I sometimes wonder what interesting story one of them is going to become for the future.

13

○ ○ ○ ○

Another Hare-Brained Idea

Mom was always telling me to stop getting hare-brained ideas like raising snakes or frogs. She couldn't figure out why I wouldn't be satisfied simply to show an interest in such creatures. Without fail I had either to raise them in a big way or not show an interest at all. Playing with normal pets was all right, but at times I also like the unusual ones.

One day I was reading a hunting and fishing magazine when an intriguing ad caught my eye. The ad read,

Wanted: People with good feel for business. Send twenty dollars for complete Worm Farm Kit and instruction materials.

Something about having my own enterprise set me into immediate action.

I was only about eight or nine years old at the time, but somehow I scrounged up twenty dollars. After secretly sending off my money in the mail, I patiently waited for something to happen.

In approximately two weeks, a large package came for me. Mother was extremely interested in the contents. I tried to hurry off to my room, but I was ordered to open the package before adult eyes. Much to my dismay, when I ripped open the box, I found only a large container filled with something that looked like shredded cardboard.

"What is that?!" Mother demanded.

"It's my worm farm, Mom," I returned.

"My God, what are you going to dream up next, Scott? Won't you ever stop these crazy ideas of yours?" she carried on.

"Come on, Mother. It's not that bad. Anyway, when I start making more money than you do at this business, you won't be so mad then," came my final retort.

With that I carried the contents of my latest endeavor off to my room for some heavy thinking and studying. I pulled out the instruction manual and started searching for the method in which to make hundreds of dollars. Everything in the manual was easy to understand. The first detail I had to take care of was finding a couple of containers for my worm farm. As with my frogs, I decided two fifty-gallon barrels, cut in half, would work the best. Next, I was instructed to pour the contents of the package I'd received equally into the two containers. I was then further instructed to add water until the cardboard paper material became moist, but not too wet. Thus far, it had been rather fun, I thought, so I couldn't wait to read on in the directions. The next move was to store the containers somewhere they would remain cool, preferably in temperatures between forty or fifty degrees. *Just great*, I thought. Where was I going to find a place that cool now that it was summertime, and the temperature was almost eighty or ninety degrees every day?

At that point, an idea struck me. Sinful though the idea was, at least it was workable. I dragged my two large, sawed-off barrels into my father's big walk-in egg cooler. After summing up the situation, I figured if Dad could be swayed into letting me carry out this idea, I would be back in business again. After all, the chickens weren't giving enough eggs to fill the entire cooler, so why not put some of the empty space to use?

At first Dad gave me some argument, but I suppose he could see a valuable lesson for me to learn, so he allowed me to carry on. Mom tried to get Dad to put a stop to my insanity, but, as if he knew something I didn't, he quieted her and said I should continue.

I remember thinking that with their support, I could finally rest easily. Once again I read further in my instruction manual. It told me to acquire some angleworms and nightcrawlers. According to the manual, one barrel was to breed and raise angleworms, and the other barrel was for nightcrawlers. Apparently, only a few of the slimy creatures were needed in each barrel for the multiplying to take place. I knew I was getting close to some real payoff, so I went hunting for some angleworms. This was the easy part, because all I did was to go to Mom's garden and dig it up a little. Before long I had about twenty worms. My complication came while trying to find nightcrawlers. I hunted and looked everywhere but couldn't find any. Dad said to go lift up some dry cow pies (which is the same as cow manure) and look for crawlers there. I looked until my hands were both black and smelly, only to come up empty handed. Mother then suggested I go out that night with a flashlight and hunt. I asked why and she replied that, during the night, the nightcrawlers came above ground. That night I looked for what seemed like hours with absolutely no luck. At last, almost in tears and ready to give in to defeat, I went to bed. Later that night as if a miracle had happened, it rained. In fact it rained so hard, the following morning our driveway was literally covered with hundreds of worms and nightcrawlers. Quick as a flash I picked out the liveliest ones and added them to my prepared breeding medium in the egg cooler.

Once again Mom started in on Dad about how disgusting it was to have worms in our egg cooler, but Dad calmed her.

The final paragraph of the manual informed me that all I had to do was moisten the medium occasionally to prevent it from drying out and watch my future profits grow.

I sat and read the paragraph again. Watch my profits grow! It finally struck me. Exactly how does one get rich on worms and nightcrawlers? The stupid manual left out the most important and relevant detail. I sat there, and felt my ears getting hot and my face getting flushed. I was glad no one was around, because I felt as though a big neon sign were flashing over my head with the word SUCKER printed on it.

In a short while, I calmed down and decided to at least play the worm farm out for a short time. A short time was all it really took, too, because the little slithery worms and crawlers multiplied like mad. In only a few days I dug around in the medium and found countless young ones. In a couple of weeks, there appeared to be thousands inside the barrels.

I was getting desperate. At this point I decided I'd better start coming up with some aggressive ideas. My first idea was to sell worms and nightcrawlers to fishermen. It was summertime, and with summer comes the fishing season. Once again, however, my idea fizzled out. Sure, Minnesota may be nicknamed the "Land of Ten Thousand Lakes," but, where our farm was located, the nearest fishing lake might as well have been a thousand miles away. It seemed as though my business was headed for bankruptcy because of a large supply and total lack of demand.

My last attempt was at a pet store. Mom drove me to the store, and I walked up to the manager like a well-bred little businessman. I asked him if he'd consider a purchase contract with me, where I raised the worms and crawlers, and he bought them to feed to the reptilian pets.

The store manager's answer most severely deflated my self-esteem. He informed me that not a single creature in his store ate worms. They all ingested some other form of food. With that, I thanked him and left.

By this time, Mom and Dad were probably getting the thrill of a life time. Mom could finally see why Dad had told her to let me proceed. If she had hampered me in the beginning, I would have been a real headache. All the warning in the world would not have taught me the lesson I was learning for myself.

I had spent my hard-earned money for something I knew nothing about. I'd put a lot of time, labor, and thinking into the "business." In the end, I had thousands of slimy, smelly worms and nightcrawlers, and I couldn't even give them away.

At last I went to Mom and begged for some advice. Seeing I was at my wits' end, Mother gave me some comforting and sound advice.

"The worm farm was an interesting idea and worth a try, Scott, but not all businesses work out. After all, Dad and I have tried different farming enterprises, and not all of them have worked," Mom stated.

"That's fine, Mom, but I spent almost all my money for this dumb idea, and now I don't know what to do," I bellyached back.

"My advice is to chalk this one up to experience, and just put the worms and nightcrawlers out in the garden or in Dad's field where they will do some good for the soil," Mom went on.

"Put them in the garden or field!" and then I paused.

I knew Mother was right and to defend myself further would gain nothing for me. I told my mother I'd get the barrels out of the egg cooler immediately. She assured me I was making the right decision, even if it did hurt somewhat.

After carrying the heavy barrels to the garden, I returned the little creatures back to the earth from which they had come.

At that time of my life, such a lesson in life was difficult to swallow. I can look back now and smile, because I realize even something as simple as an angleworm can help a person pattern his life for the better.

14

○ ○ ○ ○

The Varieties of a Pet Store

Speculating on the expenses of my upcoming college education, I started looking for a job my senior year in high school. Never before had I hunted for a job. I'd worked for area farmers while growing up, but only on an irregular basis. Most of my off-farm work had been in the form of stacking and baling hay during the summer for the neighbors. Now I had finally reached the point in my life where money had to be earned for a definite purpose, not simply for some extra spending cash.

The thought of job hunting was a frightening and virgin experience for me. As everyone who has done this unpleasant task realizes, finding a job is a trying endeavor. One must constantly analyze his own qualifications, then seek out a position he will be content with. Once a certain position is located, a person must sell himself to the maximum in hope of being hired.

My biggest hardship was locating a job I'd be happy with. I knew girls who were working as waitresses, cashiers, or secretaries. I also knew guys who worked at gas stations or stores or did janitor's work. Nothing I looked at seemed right for me. I asked the school counselor for assistance but came up with no solution. I kept watching the want ads in the paper, but it seemed as if only the hard-to-fill positions ever showed up in the paper.

The question that kept running through my mind was, "Exactly what could I do well?" I'd been a farmer all my life, so working with animals was about all I really knew. Then it struck me. In the city of Rochester was a big new shopping mall. One of the stores in the mall was a pet store. I began dreaming about the thrills of working with all the exotic pets in a store such as this.

One weekend on a Saturday, I dressed up and headed for Rochester with only the thought of a job on my mind. I strolled into the store and looked all around. There were hundreds of bubbling aquariums in the room with every size, color, and shape of fish imaginable within their watery holds. At both ends of the store was every animal one could envision. I spotted parrots, monkeys, mice, rats, hamsters, snakes, lizards, turtles, dogs, and many, many more.

After getting over my bright-eyed astonishment about the pet store, I started hunting for the owner. The store was owned by a young couple named John and Peggy. They were both in their office at the time, so one of the workers in the store directed me to their office door. I knocked, then apprehensively waited. After a brief pause, the door opened, and John said, "What can I do for you, young fella?"

"My name is Scott Gottschalk, and I was wondering if you could use any more help around your store. I'm real good with animals," I hurriedly spilled forth.

"Tell you what, Scott: Peggy and I need a break, so let's go grab a soda, and talk about it," John replied.

By this time my heart was pumping so fast, I was sure my ears were all red. I followed John and Peggy to a small cafe in the shopping mall, where he bought us all something to drink. When we were finally sitting, Peggy asked me to tell them a little about myself.

As I explained earlier, one must always sell himself when at the mercy of a potential employer. I started explaining my history, experiences, and goals to John and Peggy. When I finished, I was confident they knew enough about me to make a decision.

To my disappointment, John said he didn't need any more help, but stated I had excellent qualifications for the job. He shook hands with me and assured me of a call if he was going to hire again. I thanked both of them and dejectedly departed for home.

I was sure I'd gotten the old "heave ho" routine. That's what they always said when they wanted to get rid of someone; we'll call you if something comes along. I immediately tried locating another job, because I didn't think it was worth holding my breath for the pet-store position. Time was wasting, and I still needed a job badly.

A couple of weeks later I was still hunting for a job when the phone rang. Mom answered, then called me to the phone. It was Peggy, and she said John and she wanted to confer with me again. I asked when, and she told me as soon as I could. Almost before the receiver was in its cradle, I was changing clothes and heading toward town for another attempt at the job I'd been dreaming about. Before long I was standing before John and Peggy in gleeful anticipation of their desires.

John explained that one of his employees had left, so a position in the pet store was now available. He further stated I had been their first choice, just as he had promised, because of my excellent qualifications. John outlined the working schedule, explained some of the details of the job, quoted the wage per hour, and asked if I wanted the job. I happily accepted the position and thanked them.

The next step in the process was my training sessions. For two long weeks John put me through a rigorous training period. The job title I would be holding was pet counselor, so it was imperative to understand fully all the elements of the position. Not only was I to sell the animals and animal products within the store, but also be knowledgeable enough to counsel someone at any time.

One can well imagine the difficulty of learning the breeds and habits of hundreds of different kinds of fish, much less all the other exotic types of animals. Each day of the training session, John would teach me, then test me. He even role-played to see how I would react under different circumstances that might crop up in the store.

At long last, John informed me I was ready to hit the floor. He said he was satisfied with my understanding of the store and its products and was now interested in my performance. I confidently assured him I'd do the best possible job I could.

The first few weeks on the job posed some challenges. It took some getting used to when a customer would come in and ask for a silver dollar. This, by the way, is a fish. Other people inquired about Jack Dempseys, swordtails, or red-tailed sharks. I had to understand fully all the living as well as eating habits of these types of aquatic life. Other potential buyers would inquire about boa constrictors, baby alligators or parrots.

It was only when someone asked about a rat that I turned queasy. To me a rat was a sly, slinky, creepy creature, whether it was white or not. The other workers within the store thought I was some kind of coward when asked by a customer to put a certain rat in a container for them. Everyone else would just pick the rat up and put it in a box. I, however, would not touch a rat with my bare hands for reasons explained in an earlier chapter. I would always put on a pair of heavy, padded gloves which were used when handling biting or clawing animals. With the gloves on my hands, then, and only then, would I touch a rat.

Shortly after acquiring the pet-store job, I developed an avid hatred for one of the permanent inhabitants of the store. One of the first pets ever brought to the store was a mammoth, scarlet McCaw parrot. The parrot's name was Caw, and he was never sold, because parrots were so hard to import into our country. Scarlet McCaw parrots are one of the largest birds in the parrot family. These colorful birds can fly but are quite heavy and prefer not to fly. John had informed me if an adequate supply of food was in one tree in the wild, and no predators were about, a McCaw parrot could easily spend weeks, months, or years in the same tree. McCaw parrots also are one of the better talking parrots. Now a parrot doesn't actually talk on its own but, in reality, it mimics. With all the action in the pet store, Caw had learned to be a real "ham." His favorite vocal expression was a whistle. He could imitate the same whistle a man gives a pretty woman. Often I'd watch women walk past the big picture window where Caw was stationed. As if he knew what he was doing, Caw would wait until the women were beyond him and then whistle. More than once, I saw certain gals turn quickly around with indignant expressions on their faces. I actually think they were looking for some guy who had whistled at them.

Other expressions Caw loved were: "Hello," "How are you?" and repeating his own name. The big bird would sit on his T-stand hour after hour, day after day, whistling and talking to people. Caw probably singlehandedly brought more business to the pet store than any other animal.

I asked John one day how old Caw was. John said he was about twenty years old. I thought that was pretty old, but John said some McCaws had lived beyond eighty years of age. My next question was, what was Caw's worth. At that John gave me a figure close to two thousand dollars, but today it would be considerably higher.

Caw was a rather moody parrot. At times he would talk and draw attention to himself, and at other times he'd just sit about sulking. Sometimes I felt sorry for the big bird because he would get so bored and he would sit and pick the bright red feathers from his chest. Caw was a magnificent specimen to view, though. He was mostly bright, scarlet red with traces of blue and white on his body. The most majestic part of this bird was his tail. Caw had long, beautiful, red-and-blue tail feathers that hung well below his perch. His main feather was a full two feet long.

Only a few of the workers were allowed to handle and feed Caw. His diet consisted mainly of peanuts and sunflower seeds, which he could crack and eat like a master. One of the workers actually had Caw trained to crawl slowly up his arm, then take a peanut from his shoulder. John constantly reminded us to be careful when working with Caw. A large parrot can badly injure a person with his powerful, hooked beak. Incidentally, a parrot can crush down with five hundred pounds per square inch when clamping his mouth shut. People who have tried capturing parrots in the wild have actually lost fingers from a parrot bite.

I kept my distance from Caw for several weeks after starting my new job. I was content to watch some of my coworkers petting, feeding, and working with Caw. Finally, my curiosity got the best of me, and I went into the parrot's room one day. How interesting it would be, I thought, if Caw could crawl up my arm. I knew, though, before this could ever be attempted, I would have to gain his trust. I looked all around and no one was in sight, so I pulled a peanut out of my pocket and gently thrust it toward the parrot's powerful mouth. That was the last detail I remember before seeing red. Caw lunged out, grabbing my hand between the thumb and forefinger, and then clamped shut. His beak smacked down and broke right through my skin. "Yeeoow," I blurted out as I quickly withdrew my painful hand.

At that point, all I could see was a disgusting, ornery parrot in front of me, and all I could feel was vengeance within me as I cradled my bleeding hand. Without thinking, I reached out and yanked on the long tail of the parrot. Caw emitted the most blood-curdling squawk I've ever witnessed, as his long feather plucked loose from his hind end.

About then my senses returned, and I realized what I had done. If my bosses found out I'd pulled the parrot's beautiful tail feather out, I surely wouldn't have a job anymore. Once again I looked around, but somehow no one had spotted me as yet. As I prepared to leave the room, I struggled with what to do with the two-foot-long feather lying on the floor. Without much hesitation, I grabbed the feather, stuck it under my shirt, and left the room. I figured, with any luck, maybe John or Peggy wouldn't even notice the feather's absence. With it lying on the floor, though, they would surely suspect foul play.

No one noticed anything about the feather that day, so, when I left for home, I smuggled the feather out with me. Several of the employees asked, however, how I'd cut my hand, and I explained I had cut myself with a knife.

The following weekend John and Peggy had an employee meeting. The first item discussed, much to my dismay, was Caw. John was strictly asking for any information on Caw's missing tail feather. I sat there and tried to look as blank-faced as everyone else, because I knew my job depended on it. No one could explain why Caw's tail was suddenly more than one foot shorter in length. Finally John let the matter drop, and within a few weeks it was forgotten.

I hung Caw's gorgeous feather in my bedroom. Years later, when I was no longer an employee of the pet store, I decided to take the feather off the wall and put it to some good use. The feather was placed in my cowboy hat, and I still wear it to this day. I've been asked several times by people where I received such a unique hat feather, and I invariably repeat my story.

I do hope, however, when my former employers read about this, they can chuckle about the story and not come looking for me. After all, I paid for that feather with an extremely painful hand.

One day the store was extremely quiet, and I was getting bored. A supply of new fish had recently arrived so another employee and I were looking over the various species. I kept noticing, in several of the aquariums, a particular kind of fish that seemed out of place with the others in the tank. I asked my friend what the deal was, and he began explaining. The beautifully colored, fan-tailed fish that were scattered about in all the different tanks were called fighting betas. These fish had originally been bred in the Orient to participate in fish fights, much like dogfights or chicken fights.

"You mean, if you put these fish together in the same tank, they'll fight?" I questioned.

My friend assured me they were supposed to fight to the death. I asked him how he knew and he said he had read about them. Then I asked if he'd ever seen them fight, and he said he hadn't.

"Well, do people buy them now to fight?" I further inquired.

"Oh, no, that's illegal. Most people just buy them because they are so pretty to look at," he stated.

Almost simultaneously, he and I looked at each other with the "devil" in our eyes. We both felt, since no one was in the store, what harm could a little experiment create? We both agreed to put two fighting betas together, and, if they really did start hurting each other, we would simply separate them again.

We put two of the multicolored specimens together, then watched. The fish swam calmly around the tank with freely flowing fins, until they spotted each other. Faster than a wink, the two charged then stopped just a fraction of an inch from each other. At that point, I witnessed the most spectacular expression of living color I've ever seen. Both fish, as though driven by a hidden force, flared out their fanlike fins. This action seemed to increase their size twofold. What really amazed us though was their ability to change color. I had felt these fish were marvelously colored before, but, now, when faced by a challenger, they somehow were able to fire their colors, or make themselves much brighter.

At that precise moment the fight broke out. With bolting speed, the little fish charged each other. They rammed head on, time and time again. I had seen enough, so I quickly grabbed a net and pulled one of them from the aquarium, and dropped it into a separate tank.

As quickly as the fish had started fighting, they just as quickly settled down, and both began their peaceful flowing motion once again. Both my coworker and I agreed on the fact that these fish could indeed fight to kill. Even today, I question how anything so lovely could be so fierce.

As I progressed through the months on the job, I gained valuable experience working with both animals and people. Many times, though, I would just as soon have worked solely with the animals. People are often hard to work with, especially when their pets are involved.

One example of an always-aggravating experience was with mothers buying fish for their young children. I usually had plenty of work to do, but I would patiently wait as some youngster went from tank to tank eyeballing the hundreds of fish. Without fail, the kid would spot some guppy or another kind of fish and want a particular one. Did you ever try to pick out one particular guppy in an aquarium of perhaps three hundred guppies? Well, I can say from experience, it's extremely difficult. Whenever I would finally net the fish I was trying to capture, the child would invariably cry out, "It's the wrong one," and the process would repeat once again.

Another classical example of hard-to-work-with people were women shopping for collars for their dogs. Whenever men came in they would grab almost any collar, purchase it, and leave. The women with their miniature hounds and toy poodles were another matter. I swear these females could spend hours trying collars on their dogs, looking at prices, and deciding on what colored rhinestones would match their dog's hair color. John had told me during my training period always to stay with a customer until he (or she) had been helped and sold. Helping some lady with a poodle collar was more than I could bear. It got so bad, if I saw some woman walking toward the collar section, I'd immediately run for the opposite end of the store.

As if the dog collar and fish incidents weren't enough, one should have seen people when it came to having their dogs clipped. One of the employees, Mary, clipped and groomed dogs on a full-time basis. I felt sorry for Mary, because of the abuse she had to take. The customers usually wanted everything done just right on their mutts, but they were never satisfied. Either Mary had clipped the hair too short, too unevenly, or too long. Seldom did anyone simply thank her for a nice job and leave.

When I think about these people, I often couldn't believe the difference in attitudes between rural and urban people. The dogs on our farm never received special attention other than a good home, good food, and friendly attention. The people I associated with on the job often would come in and purchase an expensive dog sweater worth more than the total worth of their own children's clothing. By the looks of the hair on some of their kids, I doubted they ever spent nearly the time grooming their own children that they spent on their dogs.

I suppose this is the way with human nature, and it must be realized; each to his own.

The pet-store job began allowing me to start saving money. For the first time in my life, my savings account was over one hundred dollars and climbing. About that time, I got myself into a rather ironic situation.

John was an extremely shrewd and successful businessman, and for this reason I respected him greatly. I think back now and realize he was such a good businessman that he even saw to it he sold his own employees on the store's merchandise.

Not long after taking the position of Pet Counselor, I was informed that I should start raising some fish of my own. John's philosophy was that it would be easier to work with people selling and counseling them on fish if we as employees had a common interest. I did some checking, and sure enough, every single employee of the pet store had a fish aquarium in their own home filled with various types of fish.

Not wanting to be different, I purchased an attractive twenty-gallon aquarium and stand. The pain of the purchase was made somewhat easier because John allowed employee discounts on various items. Without realizing what was happening, however, I, like all the other employees, was virtually turning my paycheck right back to my employers because of an expensive hobby. All the other employees were quite competitive about their tanks. No one, including me, was content to own a few inexpensive, yet hardy, goldfish. Instead, we all had to own the most expensive, fancy, delicate fish the pet store could provide. On several occasions I took home fish that were over ten dollars apiece in price. Generally, these fish were the first to die once at home. My aquarium, though, was the talk of all my friends and neighbors in our little rural community, because it was filled with so many rare and exotic fish.

I suppose the statement "One thing leads to another" aptly described me on my next project.

Dr. Sitapong was an Oriental doctor working at the Mayo Clinic in Rochester. During the previous few years, he had spent literally thousands of dollars on his fish hobby. Whenever he would stop in the store after working at the clinic, he'd walk up to me and say, "Have you got any new species of fish in today, Scott?"

Usually on each shipment of fish, one or two different species were included, so I would direct Dr. Sitapong to the new arrivals. Most of the time, the doctor would leave with a fish in a container under his arm.

I knew from talking with other employees, Dr. Sitapong had originally started out with freshwater fish, but was now going toward saltwater fish. Freshwater fish are more hardy than saltwater species, but the beauty and color of saltwater varieties are unmatched. Word had it that Dr. Sitapong had approximately fifteen large aquariums in his dwelling.

To switch from all freshwater fish to saltwater would have been a huge financial endeavor. For starters, saltwater aquariums can have no metal parts, metal filters, or metal air pumps because of the corrosive actions of the salt. The equipment alone is highly expensive. The other matter is the tremendous expense of the beautifully colored, but delicate, saltwater varieties of fish, which had to be transported from great distances.

Dr. Sitapong's goal was in fact to convert completely to saltwater, because one day he stopped by the pet store and posed an interesting question to me.

"Scott, I want to convert my last freshwater tank to saltwater, but I don't know what to do with the two fish in the tank. You see, they are wild piranha, and I have to be careful who gets them. Would you be interested?" asked the doctor.

I knew from my training sessions with John, piranha were a hard-to-come-by fish as of lately. Our government had shut down importation of wild piranha a few years earlier, because certain people had done some risky things. Evidently, some Florida and California piranha owners had gotten sick of their pets and disposed of them, either by flushing down the toilet or by other means. In any event, some people had been fishing in streams in Florida and California and actually caught piranha. It certainly doesn't take much imagination to see the repercussions of piranha starting to breed in the more tropical parts of our country. Our government shut down the importation of wild piranha as soon as the discovery was made. From then on, the only piranhas available to sell were aquarium-bred, domestic species.

The piranha is a relatively small, pan-type fish, with a bulldog face. Within their jaws are masses of razor-sharp teeth that can rip and bite through just about anything. The fish is generally only six to eight inches in length, and many nightmare stories have been told about how large animals had fallen into piranha-infested waters, only to be eaten to the bone within minutes by these carnivores.

I sat for a few moments thinking about Dr. Sitapong's suggestion. If he really did have a couple of the last wild piranha to come into our country, then they would surely be unique pets to own.

"Sure, I'd love to have them," I finally said. "How much are you asking?"

"Oh, I don't want money, Scott, I will gladly give the fish to you," replied the doctor.

I most joyfully thanked him, and we set up a date on which I could come to his place and pick the fish up.

My next task was to locate another aquarium. I really didn't want to spend all the money necessary to purchase a new setup, so I started asking around for a used aquarium. At last, one of the pet store's employees said he had a thirty-gallon tank he would sell me for about half-price.

When at last I had the aquarium set up in my house, I went to Dr. Sitapong's place with a big metal bucket and a net. As I rapped on the doctor's door, I could hear the muffled sound of many air pumps sending bubbles through water. It was as though I were in the pet store again judging from the sounds coming from behind the door.

At last Dr. Sitapong opened the door and let me enter. Never before had I seen so many beautiful, large aquariums filled with saltwater fish. The sight of his wonderful hobby almost put me in a trance as I glanced from tank to tank.

"The piranhas are over here, Scott," called the doctor.

My eyes widened as I looked at the two toothy specimens within the tank. Both piranhas were the red-breasted variety, which is notoriously known as the most deadly of the species. Each fish was about six inches long and swam cautiously around the tank with an evil look in his eyes.

We filled the bucket with water from the aquarium, then transferred the fish into the bucket. I once again thanked the doctor for his generosity and departed.

When at home, I quickly added the fish to their new home I had so carefully prepared. I had made the inside of the aquarium look somewhat like a prehistoric scene. I had placed in the tank large pieces of petrified wood, surrounded by plastic plants. In the center of the aquarium, I had placed a large, plastic, human skull and then channeled a hidden air hose to emit bubbles from the skull's mouth.

With the two new inhabitants in place, my fish hobby had finally set me apart from my other coworkers at the pet store. No one at the store owned piranha!

The following year was an interesting and educating one with my dangerous fish. To begin with, their appetites were horrendous. A piranha usually will devour only live food. Since I was working at the pet store, this didn't really create much of a problem. My boss said each night when I went home after work, I could sort through the different fish tanks and take home any sick or dying fish for my piranha. This worked out well. The time came, however, when I stopped working at the pet store and was faced with a problem. Buying fish from a pet store to feed piranha is expensive if you aren't an employee. I finally started buying about a dozen minnows each week from a bait shop, and this kept my hungry fish content. Occasionally I'd throw them a piece of ham, chicken, or steak and they would happily ingest it. I even tried experimenting by feeding the piranha worms. This didn't work well, though. The fish would suck a worm into its mouth like a piece of spaghetti, taste it, then spit it out immediately.

Not only was the feeding interesting, but so was cleaning the piranha tank. I was never able to find a mechanical method suitable for the cleaning process, so I did the process by hand. Actually the only cleaning I did was scraping the inside of the glass to free it from algae and occasionally cleaning the gravel in the bottom of the aquarium.

The piranha usually shied to a far corner of the tank when someone was directly in front, so I decided to clean the tank one day with the flesh-eaters still inside. I usually removed them, but felt it was worth a try just once.

I cautiously stuck my hand in the water of the aquarium, and, to my surprise, the piranha backed farther into the far corner. Feeling smarter, I buried my arm to the elbow and began cleaning the sides of the aquarium. All at once, one piranha made a dashing bolt directly at my arm. I vividly remember screaming in fright and withdrawing my arm so quickly I pulled half the water in the tank out onto the carpet.

After that occurrence, I never again risked the tissue on my arm to clean the aquarium. Instead, I simply removed my dangerous fish first.

One day I went to look at my aquariums, and one of the piranhas was badly injured. I had heard somewhere, if not given enough room, piranha will attack each other. One piranha had bitten the lower jaw of the other almost completely off. Because of its injury, I had to dispose of the injured fish.

The time finally arrived when I had to sell my fish and aquarium so I could move to St. Paul for my college work.

I, like Dr. Sitapong, was apprehensive of the next owner of my piranha. I decided to contact the biology department at the community college in Rochester. I said I'd donate my remaining piranha to them, if they would take good care of it. They agreed that they would, so I relinquished my last and favorite fish.

In all, my working days at the pet store were cherished ones. The experiences gave me another perspective on a different form of the animal world. Certainly not all the times were good, but they all had a part in my animal entourage.

15

○ ○ ○ ○

A Crazy Cattle Dog

Not so many years ago, a strange breed of dog surfaced in our country. The first people to start raising the dogs were mainly livestock farmers and ranchers. The peculiar breed of dog was an Australian blue heeler or Queensland blue heeler.

Heelers, as they were named for short, did in fact come from Australia. The origin of the blue heeler dog came as the result of an odd mating. These dogs were the result of a cross between a shepherd dog and the wild dog of Australia. The wild dogs were called Australian dingos, and they still roam Australia in packs, just as wolves do.

Heelers were first discovered in Australia as working dogs. Their ability to herd sheep, cattle, or other livestock went almost unchallenged. Blue heelers got their name for two reasons. Generally, these dogs are tinted blue. Actually, the way the white blends into the gray hair on their coats often gives them a blue appearance. The "heeler" part of their name is derived from their particular method for livestock persuasion. A balking cow or sheep is usually more than happy to oblige a lightning fast nip in the heels by a blue heeler.

A blue heeler is only a small-to-medium sized dog. They have a slight similarity to an undersized German shepherd dog. Although these fairly small dogs lack immense size, they certainly have strength, speed, heart, and courage.

Years ago, at one of the first cattle shows Jerry and I participated in, I had my first introduction to a blue heeler. My brother and I had been casually walking down the rows of beef cattle at the fair, when suddenly I spotted a different-looking dog. Pete was the dog's owner and a friend of mine, so I asked about the dog. Pete informed me his dog's name was Blue, and he was one of the first heelers in the state. After giving Jerry and me a full rundown on Blue's history, we stared in awe at the dog.

Pete put on a demonstration for us. As he led some of his cattle out of their stalls, he said, "Get 'em, Blue." In a flash, Blue darted for first the one heel of the animal, then nipped quickly at the other heel, before the beef animal could kick out. Once in a while, a powerful hind leg would sail forth, but Blue would react magnificently by quickly retreating. I asked Pete how he had trained Blue to do such tricks, and he told me it was naturally bred in. Evidently, blue heelers have an inborn instinct to work livestock, but they must be trained to obey their masters on command.

I further learned that day a full-blooded blue heeler does very little barking. Like their solemn dingo ancestors, the heelers perform in silence. A blue heeler will bark if he is extremely excited, but, by preference, these dogs have been trained to remain silent while working livestock. The main reason was to prevent stampeding or frightening of other animals.

From the first time I set eyes on Blue, I was amazed by his capabilities. Pete informed me of another one of Blue's interesting capabilities, which I witnessed that day.

Blue heelers are perhaps one of the most powerful and trenchant dogs in their size classification. In most cases, if a heeler gets into a dogfight with another dog, size will have little to do with the final outcome.

"Blue can take any dog at this fair," Pete bragged. "He may be good, but I bet he can't take a German shepherd!" I hounded.

About then a large, unattended dog strolled into the barn and made its way toward us. I had a hidden feeling about then, Blue was going to show me a lesson I'd remember.

When Blue spotted the other dog, the hair on his back stood up. The heeler was tied to a post with a heavy rope leash and rope collar. All of a sudden, Blue lunged forward in anger at the other dog's uninvited presence, and his collar snapped in half. I stood there in disbelief. I'd never seen a dog with enough strength to break a rope of that thickness. I checked the rope out, and it hadn't been chewed on or frayed, but had simply been broken by the dog's sheer power. I started understanding why it is said that "big things come in small packages!" Any other dog would have broken its neck with a jolt such as Blue had just taken.

The next details I remember were the two dogs squaring off. I was waiting for the usual, stiff-legged walk, and POW, Blue attacked. Blue put on the quickest, most vicious exhibition of snarls and flashing fangs I'd ever seen. In seconds, the large dog was running as fast as he could for safety. Blue just calmly returned to the post he had been tied to and lay down.

Pete boastfully informed me of his dog's unequaled fighting ability. He explained how Blue often acted just as though the wild dog in his blood were coming to the surface. I had to admit, I'd never seen a domestic canine act in quite the way Blue had on that day.

Several months later Pete called me on the phone and informed me Blue was a father. Apparently Pete had mated Blue with another purebred blue heeler, and the pups had been born. I realized at that moment I wanted a pup out of Blue quite badly. For many months after witnessing Blue's tremendous abilities, Jerry and I had dreamed of owning our own special cattle dog.

Pete had given Jerry and me permission to purchase the pick of the female heeler's litter. After the usual time had passed and the puppies were ready to be weaned, my brother and I went to choose our dog.

As Jerry and I stooped to pet the short, fat, funny-looking puppies, a twinkle came to my eye as I saw a lone puppy come running from behind the barn. Up to the pack he ran, biting and nipping his way to the front where the most attention was being dealt out. I picked up the little guy saying, "Boy, aren't you a little spitfire?"

Before I knew it, I was paying Pete for the pup and loading Spit into the vehicle for our trip back to the farm.

Spit took to his new surroundings immediately. In no time at all he had lost his puppy clumsiness and was developing into a fine young heeler.

From the beginning, Spit showed an uncanny desire to chase the cattle on our farm. For many months, though, I held him back, because a well-placed kick at that stage of his life might have proved fatal, or, at the least, a kicking blow might have deterred his cattle working instincts. For this reason, I waited patiently for Spit to grow into a quick, instinctive, intelligent dog.

The day finally came when Spit was old enough to work cattle safely. I had Jerry lead one of our young beef heifers around the yard, and I walked in back of the heifer with Spit commanding, "Get her, Spit!" At first Spit cocked his head to one side and stared blatantly at me, then the heifer. He probably thought, *What are these clowns doing?* At last, however, he sprang forward, nipped the heifer in the leg, and sprang back again. I quickly lavished Spit with rewarding pats, and reassuring vocal statements. Again we started the process. Each time Spit picked up a bit more confidence and in no time was giving the beef heifer more than she had bargained for.

In the following days and weeks, Jerry and I worked with Spit at every opportunity. He was soon capable of sorting out any animal we would point a finger at. Spit would, on command, run into a group of cattle, sort out a chosen one, and bring it away from the rest. It wasn't long before I impressed my friends in much the same way Pete had impressed me with Blue on a previous occasion.

It's hard to really describe the actions of a blue heeler. These dogs always seem so full of steam. From Spit's very beginning on our farm, he was full of excess energy. My family was used to the normal functions of a "dog's life," from past farm dogs. As one well knows, most dogs like to lie around much of the time, with an occasional bark if a car drives in. Spit, on the contrary, was never caught lying about. I swear he was on the go a hundred percent of the time. If Jerry or I weren't doing chores, Spit would be out working cattle on his own. He loved racing around chasing calves and cows. Never would he bark, but he silently pestered each and every animal until they all held a most deep respect for his presence.

During the years Spit was a part of my life and a member of our farm, he charted the way for many interesting stories.

One of Spit's favorite tricks was to antagonize my father's Holstein bull calf. At the time Dad had started milking cows again in addition to raising our beef herd, so he was growing a young bull so he could service his cows. Many times I'd walk by the bull calf's pen and see Spit chasing him around, nipping at his heels. The calf, with pure terror in his eyes, would scamper from end to end in hope of fleeing from the awful dog. As the bull calf grew larger and larger, Spit continued his pranks on the bull. The bull maintained a continual fear of Spit.

Years later, long after Spit was dead and gone, the big Holstein bull remained on our farm breeding my father's dairy animals. As most generally happens; the over-two thousand-pound giant of a bull started getting mean. For years, no one had trusted him, so we invariably kept our eye on the bull and kept our distance. The bull finally got to the point where he would go through fences in his fits of anger. Whenever we had to handle the bull, though, we would take along our new dog. The new dog really didn't like cattle, and he, therefore, refused to work them. As long as the dog stayed by our side, though, the big bull was like a pussycat. Dad, Jerry, and I would laugh endlessly when that big bull would take off like a scared rabbit every-time he'd see a dog. Whether it was a big dog or small dog, all the bull could envision was his calfhood nightmares about Spit's picking on him.

Thanks to Spit's long-lasting effects, we were always able to semi-control the bull.

Spit was hyperactive and loved being on the move. A habit he picked up early in life was racing our pickup truck out of the driveway and up the road. Approximately one-quarter of a mile away from the main buildings of the farm, we had some buildings in which Dad raised beef cattle. Each day as Jerry and I did our chores, Spit would repeat the same activities. We would start the pickup and back it out of the driveway. As we backed, Spit would circle around and around the truck, going at breakneck speeds. Each time Spit would round the front end of the pickup, he'd grab onto one of the front tires with his teeth and growl. I had given up trying to break him of the annoying habit. It was as though Spit were trying to have a competition with the truck every time we drove it to do chores. Spit never chased cars, tractors, or other trucks, but, if we drove our pickup truck, he'd go crazy. Several times I jumped out of the truck and spanked him to put a damper on his annoying tricks, but the dog would, at all times, begin again. Once on the road, either Jerry or I would accelerate the vehicle, and Spit would take off, running. No matter how fast we'd drive, Spit could beat us to the buildings every time.

Before we could ever get out of the truck, Spit would run and sneak into the barn from the rear. As Jerry and I opened the door, Spit would invariably be on the other side with a trick to play.

Spit's three favorite pranks were rather humorous. One trick was that he'd wait until a person had just opened the door, then, with deep growls, Spit would jump out from nowhere and bite the door. Another of his capers occurred at the precise moment one set foot in the dark doorway of the barn. Spit would lunge out, grab one's pant leg, snarl, then shake his head viciously back and forth. Spit's last main escapade was to jump on the bales of hay at about head level, just behind the door. As Jerry and I walked into the barn, Spit would let loose, and scare us to death.

To my brother and me, these activities were like a game. I generally thought is was fun to see which caper Spit was going to try on a given day.

One time my brother and I had just raced Spit to the beef barn, and, as usual, he had disappeared behind the barn. The feed-delivery man had just dropped off some feed and was opening the door at the same time we drove up to the barn. Suddenly the feed man screamed and slammed the door shut. With a terrified expression on his face, the delivery man informed there was a wild dog behind the door. Jerry and I started laughing almost uncontrollably.

"What happened?" I somehow sounded through my laughter.

"I opened the door, and a dog jumped forward, growling viciously. It attacked the door, but I think it was going for me. Most likely it has rabies," expressed the still-shaken man.

Finally, with tears in my eyes from laughing so hard, I explained what had happened. To begin with, Spit would never have bitten anyone, and, secondly, I informed him Spit had thought it was only Jerry or me opening the door.

It had just so happened he'd opened the barn door at about the same time we usually had.

Even after thoroughly explaining the situation, the feed-delivery man was extremely cautious from that time on. My family would often catch him thrusting the door open, then jumping back in fear of Spit. In reality, though, Spit never bothered the man again.

Although I knew blue heelers had actual wild-dog blood in them, I often thought Spit had more wild characteristics than other heelers I'd seen. On several occasions I had spotted Spit roaming around the brushier parts of our farm, as though he were stalking for prey. To my astonishment, I witnessed an incredible chase by Spit one day.

As everyone knows, a rabbit is an extremely fast creature. Many times in my life, I've seen our other farm dogs scare up a rabbit, then chase after it. Without fail, however, the speeding, darting bunny would easily dodge our dogs. On a separate occasion, Spit scared up a rabbit, only this time the results were different. The rabbit sped off, full speed ahead, with Spit right behind it. Normally a rabbit can outmaneuver a larger, more awkward dog. Each time the rabbit cornered, Spit cornered just as gracefully. Before my unbelieving eyes, Spit captured the rabbit and then proceeded to eat it. I'd never witnessed such an act of the wild from a dog before.

I saw Spit accomplish some other unbelievable stunts as well. Adjacent to our house was a grove of evergreen trees. In the spring of the year, pesty blackbirds are all about our farm. Spit would crouch low at the base of the trees. On two occasions, I saw him jump into the air and capture low-flying blackbirds before they could get into the trees. I remember thinking more than once to myself about how old Tippy had constantly tried to scare off the birds, but Spit actually did get rid of them.

For years Jerry, Dad, and I took Spit along with us to cattle shows. He was definitely a well-traveled canine.

Whenever we started loading our beef animals into the trailer for some distant cattle show, Spit would get all excited. When we were ready to depart, Spit would jump into the truck, and off we'd drive to a show.

Spit served three purposes for us at a cattle show. In addition to his friendly company, he never hesitated to follow behind our cattle as we led them. He made sure there was never any balking. Any hesitant animal invariably received a quick, well-placed nip by Spit. Our dog's other main purpose while at a show was as a watchdog. It is a well-known fact at a cattle show, thieves occasionally like to steal one's belongings while one is in the show ring. We would simply tie Spit to our equipment box while away, and Spit always kept a watchful eye on all our belongings.

Intriguing, funny, helpful, and mysterious are all adjectives that described Spit. He could be any or all of those descriptions if he wanted to. Courageous was a separate description, which I felt really explained Spit.

One day a pen of about ten steers broke down their fence and escaped. I was doing chores that evening with my faithful dog at my side, when I detected the problem. I quickly ran for Dad, and in moments we were patching up the fence. The next step was to find the steers. Dad and I searched briefly and before long found the delinquent steers holding up in the thick mass of evergreen trees in our grove.

Dad told me to go in and bring them out, but, try as I might, I couldn't push through the thick growth. Each time I tried I would get a sharp branch in the face. At last I decided to let Spit attempt to bring them out. "Sic 'em, Spit," I shouted, and without hesitation, the courageous dog sprang into the thicket.

Dad and I heard snarling as well as growling, and all at once Spit emitted a horrible scream and came flying through the air from the thick trees. Evidently the steers had ganged up on him and one or several of them had kicked him. Poor Spit had been smashed in his mouth and was injured. Two of the dog's teeth were kicked out, and his tongue was bleeding quite badly where he had bitten into it. Dad and I were positive Spit would give up, but he rushed quickly back into the trees. He must have been really mad, because, all at once, as if thunder were sounding, the whole group of steers came running out. Almost every steer had bloodstains on his hind legs where Spit had bitten him with his injured and bleeding mouth. The dog continued chasing the troublesome bunch until they were safely in their pen again. I gained a true respect for Spit that day.

Spit had been on our farm for five years and had been a great asset to us. Due to the hazards of his style of working cattle, Spit had many teeth knocked out. Scattered throughout his set of teeth were many open spots, but even in pain Spit had never subsided.

Spit had been chasing Jerry and me in the pickup while going to do chores for so many years, we almost didn't notice his antics anymore. One slippery, snowy, wintery day, my brother and I hopped in the truck as we had done daily for years. As usual, Spit started running around the truck and biting the front tires, just as he had always done. Jerry backed the pickup truck around and started forward. Suddenly the truck bounced up slightly as though we'd run over something, and I said, "I didn't see any chunk of ice in the road."

"Neither did I," said Jerry, "I wonder what it was."

At that moment we spotted a terrible sight. After all those years of playing his game, Spit had blown it. Either he had gotten too slow in his older age, or else he had slipped on the ice, but at any rate, we had just run over our dog.

We both jumped out of the cab and ran to Spit's side. Blood was coming from his mouth and his eyes were all glazed. I almost started crying as I lifted Spit's mangled body and carried him to the house. Both his legs were shattered, his shoulder was broken and one of his lungs had probably collapsed because he could hardly breathe.

As Spit lay there, lingering on, I realized nothing could possibly save our faithful friend, and I couldn't bear to see him suffering. Finally, I went and got my gun, loaded it, and returned to Spit's side. With the heaviest heart I've ever felt, I said good-bye to Spit, put the barrel of a gun to his head, closed my tearing eyes, and squeezed the trigger. When I opened my eyes, Spit was at last out of pain and still.

Spit had been a wonderful helper and a good friend. He may have died rather harshly, but he lived a good, full life. Jerry and I agreed that day, that if Spit could have chosen a way to die, he would have preferred to go out in style, just as he did.

Dogs like Spit are hard to replace when they pass on, but they are never forgotten in the hearts of a true animal lover.

16

○ ○ ○ ○

Urban Cowboy

"My God, someone has stolen my motorcycle!" I screamed out loud. "This city makes me sick. None of the neighbors speak to one another, and no one seems to care if a person even exists."

I'd only been in St. Paul for two weeks trying to adjust to college life, and my eyes were faced with a rude awakening. How I had regretted leaving my family, farm, and animal friends in the first place. Never before had I been forced to abandon all my beloved secure items at once. Even though the decision had been hard, I had opted to pack my belongings, and take up a four-year residency in the city I'd chosen for my college degree in Animal Science.

One morning during the second week of school, I came outside my apartment only to find the chain cut on my motorcycle, which had been secured to a post. The shock was almost unbearable. My motorcycle had been a relatively large-sized road bike, and evidently some professional thieves had simply loaded it during the night, then sped off. Without hesitation, I started knocking on one apartment door after another, inquiring whether anyone had spotted some peculiar action during the night. To my total astonishment, I received nothing but we-don't-care-to-get-involved attitudes from everyone I questioned.

I suddenly felt backed into a corner. The city was frightening, college was terrifying, my financial situation was weak, and I didn't know where to turn. How I longed to sit down next to a friendly, loving animal, and feel the warmth of its body and softness of its hair. I had grown up with the comfort of a presence of many animals, and, even thought they couldn't communicate verbally, the therapy these animals provided was without measure.

With all that was taking place, I finally decided I had better find a job at least to rid my mind of some of my fears. In talking with my adviser at college, I found out the various animal-research facilities hired students. Since I was studying on the Agriculture Campus, a job in one of the animal facilities seemed appropriate. I spent one afternoon looking over the swine barn, poultry barn, sheep barn, horse barn, beef barn and dairy barn. At last I decided to try for a position in the beef barn.

After giving the person in charge of the beef barn my qualifications, I awaited his comment. He stated my credentials were good, but, since there was little to do in the beef barn except clean a few pens, he wouldn't need more than the two students already working at the barn.

Completely depressed, I left the office to ponder on another potential job. My next actions found me in the office of the research dairy barn talking with the manager and assistant managers. Once again I reviewed my qualifications with the men. This time, however, instead of expressing my beef experience, I concentrated on my dairying background.

Before I knew what had happened, the job was mine, and I was asked to start work immediately. As fate had it, the dairy barn ended up being the ideal place for me to work for several reasons. Because of the large herd size and because of an almost unlimited supply of work available, over twenty students were employed. We could work just about as often or as seldom as we chose. Our schedules for work could be set up for mornings or afternoons, depending on how we wanted to work around our schooling and studies. Another important factor for me was the higher wages paid for dairy-barn employees. Evidently the pay scale was higher because of the early time of day the cows had to be milked. Outrageous as it may seem, we had to milk the cows at the early hour of 3:00 A.M. The basic reason for this hour was so the main chores could be finished before classes started later in the morning.

For nearly four years I worked an average of thirty-eight hours per week at the barn. I usually started work at three in the morning, worked until eleven, then scurried off to classes. In addition to working on school days, I worked many weekends. The rigorous working schedule, though, often took its toll on me. I occasionally dozed off right during a lecture. At night I would come back to my apartment so tuckered out all I could do was eat my supper and go to bed.

My job allowed me to completely work my way through school, and, when I did finally graduate, I was proud to say I had put myself through college without help from anyone. More important, however, than the financial aspects of the job were the animal and people experiences. The times I had with various friends I worked with and the animals within the barn are cherished moments embedded deep in my memory.

One of the details I remember was my incessant urge to clown around when the work was done at the barn. My favorite trick was to ride various animals. For as long as I could remember, I've chosen risky methods to entertain myself. Even when I was quite young, I'd ask my brother if he dared me to jump on a beef cow's back or even sometimes the bull. Jerry invariably knew I would anyway, but he would dare me just the same. I would sneak up to a cow peacefully eating at a feed bunk, spring onto her back, and away we would go. Whether I had hopped on a cow's back or a bull, the ride was usually thrilling. I often attributed my lack of getting hurt to the fact I was never afraid or tense; therefore, I took less chance of injury if smacked up.

When it started getting dull around the dairy barn, I'd begin my old tricks all over again. After spending years at perfecting my technique on wilder, rougher, beef cattle, I was sure riding dairy cattle would be much less challenging. To draw some attention, I'd first question a fellow worker as to whether he felt I could ride a particular cow out of the barn as we were turning them outside. Without fail, the dare would be set, and up I'd jump on a cow's back. The surprised cow would speed away, and I would have to worry more about being knocked in the head by the water pipes than actually getting thrown from the cow. As soon as the cow and I reached the barnyard, I would jump off, and she would turn around with puzzlement in her eyes. After livening the morning up a little, I always felt better and was then prepared to work harder.

It was not long, though, before the cow-riding bored me, so I began looking for more excitement. Each day, after the dairy herd had been given their morning exercise outside, the year-old heifers were given a chance to frolic outside. As I watched the heifers run about, I knew it would be a true accomplishment to mount one of them. I entered the enclosed lot, started racing after one of the heifers, got close enough, then leaped onto her back. About then all hell broke loose, because she started bucking and running at a tremendous speed. I clung to her as long as I possibly could, then released my leg clasp, and went flying through the air right smack into the barn wall. The collision stung a bit, but the aftermath provided reward enough to hamper the pain. Not only were Vern, Brian, and Aaron, my coworkers, standing there applauding, but I'd drawn an appreciative audience elsewhere as well. Across the street, in full view of the barnyard was the U of M Veterinary Clinic. Evidently someone had passed the word in the building about my antics, because behind just about every window were people clapping their hands in appreciation of my humorous showing. After giving a distinguished bow, I turned around, went back in the barn, and started working again.

On yet another occasion, I opted for more thrills and excitement. Adjacent to the dairy barn was the bull barn. Inside were ten of the meanest, ugliest, most ornery Holstein bulls one could ever come across. The bulls were used on an experimental basis for artificial insemination. They were individually stalled in thick, concrete dividers and chained by the necks to massive poles in their mangers.

It was our job as employees to feed and bed the bulls. Every time one entered the barn, each bull would bellow out, paw, shake its head, and carry on. There was never a doubt as to what any one of the bulls would have done to a person, had he broken loose from his stall.

One day a friend and I were doing our chores in the bull barn. Aaron was bedding and cleaning the stalls from behind the bulls, and I was feeding them from the front. I cautiously dropped chunks of hay in front of each bull. Suddenly one of the bulls reached forward as far as he could and smashed his potentially lethal head into my arm. In a flash, I jumped over the cement divider and onto the bull's massively muscled back. My purpose was twofold. I not only wanted to teach the temperamental bull a lesson but also wanted the thrill of riding a Holstein bull.

At first I felt I had acted in haste, and had made an unsafe decision. The huge beast started kicking, stomping, snorting, bucking and bellowing. Never before had he been sat on, and, if given his way, it would never happen again. I sat there in anger and fear at the bull's pent-up aggressiveness. First I started screaming at him, then I started putting my heels into his ribs. The ride reminded me of an earthquake. The main jolts were powerful and violent, but the aftershocks were mere mild tremors. The bull temper finally subsided, and, when at last he was simply quivering, I dismounted. I was a bit amazed at the shakiness of my legs when I first stood on them again. Aaron said he couldn't get over what a crazy fool I was, and we both laughed as we finished our chores.

Vern and I both started working at the barn about the same time. We were farm kids trying to work our way through school. It didn't take long before we had formed a true camaraderie between us. Vern and I often worked the same shifts, and loved to have good, fun competition. We often bragged that, as a team, we could milk the over-hundred cow herd faster than anyone else, yet get more milk from the cows. When milking, we would hurry as fast as we could in hope of getting done before each other. If Vern beat me, he'd jokingly say, "Did you have problems today, Scott?" Likewise, if I finished before Vern, I would repeat the same phrase.

It's now been years since my college education, but my friendship with Vern and my other friends still carry on.

Brian was another buddy I often worked with. It was Brian, in fact, who trained me in on the job. We worked and went to school together for years. Each time Brian and I worked, we would pull a different prank on each other. A common trick we played was calmly to walk up to each other and pour a bucket of water onto the other as he worked. Generally, if Brian first poured water on me, I'd retaliate later. There were times when we carried on for days. If I got a bucket on my clothes from Brian, I'd go to his locker, pull out his undershorts, and then drop them in the toilet. Without getting excited, Brian would take one of my gloves and fill it with cow manure. I would carry the prank on later when Brian was in the shower. As soon as he'd step into the shower, I would pull out a hose and spray him down with ice-cold water. We went on often for a week at a time, but finally he or I would call a truce. The truce was somehow always broken, because, before long, we'd be back to our playful pranks again.

Working at the barn while attending college was a tremendous experience for me. Experiments I helped perform still benefit me to this day while I farm on my own. The barn provided a home-type situation for me, and more than once it helped me make it through some difficult times.

About halfway through my college days, I decided to join the university's Rodeo Club. Many times I'd watched rodeos, either on television or in person, but never had I participated in a rodeo. The first meeting I went to, I was somewhat frightened by the tall, lanky, tough-looking club members. They talked freely about broken bones, sprained joints, and so forth. The reason I had decided to join the club was to see if rodeoing was similar to the kinds of things I'd done with my ponies, horses, and cattle-riding.

The Rodeo Club was in the process of setting up a rodeo, which was to be held at the State Fair Coliseum. The other members asked me what I wanted to participate in at the rodeo. I informed them I'd never done any rodeo activities before, but I thought I'd try bull-riding and steer-wrestling. They all chuckled and said I'd need some lessons as well as practice first. The club had a mechanical bucking machine that could simulate a bucking bull. Many times I crawled onto the machine, shook my head to begin the ride, and hung on. More times than not, however, the machine's operator could send me flinging through the air and onto the hard ground.

The club members told me I would have to enroll in a steer-wrestling rodeo school if I was to have any chance at all in the event. They informed me that this event involved technique almost more than any other factor.

The next detail I remember was skipping college for a couple of days and driving many miles to a retired professional cowboy's ranch in hopes of learning how to steer-wrestle.

Vick was the typical stereotype of a cowboy, tall, husky, and calloused looking. He looked me over and asked how big I was. I told him I was five feet nine inches tall, and weighed a hundred and sixty-five pounds.

"Kind of puny, aren't you, boy, to be trying this?" he asked.

"I've been throwing our beef calves around for years, and that didn't bother me," I returned.

Vick said I was a bit small to be throwing four to six hundred-pound longhorn steers, but, with proper technique I might fare all right. He then went on to tell me about all the rodeos he had won, and the thrills he'd had.

My first lesson involved standing next to the chute with the steer and grabbing the longhorn correctly when it was released. Vick said a steer could be dropped like a fly if it were done properly. To make a qualifying throw, one must either stop the animal's forward progress or change its direction. The latter is the best, because steer wrestling is a timed event, and, by changing direction, the steer can actually be thrown before he has stopped moving.

The next series of instructions was learning how to dismount from a speeding horse onto a speeding steer, without committing suicide.

It most certainly is a scary feeling to be dangling from the side of a rapidly running horse.

When at last all the proper methods of the sport were drilled into my head, the time came to actually try the sport. Vick released steer after steer. I chased each one with the horse, dropped off, and continually missed, fell, or was relentlessly dragged all about the arena. Finally, after about thirty attempts, I grabbed a steer properly by the horns and threw it. I was ecstatic.

By the end of the day I was bruised, scraped, cut, sore, and tired. I had ripped the bottom of my cowboy boot completely off. All was not in vain, though, because Vick said I showed real promise.

The day finally came for the big rodeo. I paid my entry fee for the bull-riding and steer-wrestling events. I remember walking around the various pens of livestock long before the start of the rodeo, wondering which bull or steer I would have to compete against that day.

All my friends from the dairy barn and from college came to the rodeo. My first event was steer-wrestling, and I borrowed another club member's horse for the event. I nodded my head, the steer took off, and the horse and I followed close behind. To my astonishment, I found myself perfectly positioned on the steer's head. The main problem, though, was that I had drawn a big six-hundred pound steer, and his forward momentum kept dragging me forward. At last I halted him, and while the adrenalin surged in my blood, the steer thundered to the ground. I stood up with a true sense of accomplishment welling up inside my chest. I had dropped the steer in sixteen seconds. This was a long way from a winning performance, but, as I was told later, not many contestants ever compile a time at all in their first try. My time placed me eighteenth out of twenty-five contestants, so I was left with a triumphant feeling.

My emotions soon settled, because the bull-riding event was next. For a long time, rodeo bull-riding has been considered as the most dangerous sport on earth. Other sports such as football are rough, but a ton of bone-crushing Brahma bull can do more damage to a human being than a whole football team.

I had drawn a coal-black Brahma named Midnight Demon. By the time I was settling down on the bull's broad back, my hands were dripping with perspiration. As I wrapped the cinch rope tightly about my left hand, the bull started breathing hard. His devilish eyes kept looking back at me, and I knew his main desire was to rid his back of me, then kill me if possible. My Rodeo Club friends warned me to be running before I hit the ground, or else the bull would surely hook me with his awesome and deadly horns.

As I think back, it seems odd, but I never once questioned why I was doing such a crazy stunt. Instead, I concentrated only on trying to stay with the bull for an eight-second qualifying time.

At last I took a deep breath, said okay to the gate man, and off I went. I can assure you, I thought I was riding a container of exploding dynamite. The bull bucked and spun first around to this left, then altered his direction and spun to his right. I hung tight for approximately five seconds; then I could hang on no longer. The bull sent me sailing through the air. I landed on my rear, bounced up like a ball, and dashed to safety. People often laugh and say five seconds isn't very long, but, on a Brahma bull, seconds seem more like hours.

I obviously didn't place in the bull-riding competition, and, because of what happened to the rider after me, I decided never to bull-ride again.

Before I could stop my knees from shaking, the next fellow came out of the chute on the bull. He was also evicted from the bull's back, but instead of being thrown clear as I had been, he fell beneath the bull's hooves. In a flash, I listened and watched as the massive weight of the bull's hind legs came crushing into the head and neck area of the man. I heard the loud snap of a bone. The bull then whirled on the, by then, unconscious man and started ramming him with its head. At last, the bull was driven off, and the ambulance rushed out. As they loaded his limp body onto the stretcher, I could see the blood oozing from his mouth. At that instant I knew I would never try rodeo bull-riding again. The man was lucky, because he didn't die, but he suffered a severe concussion and a compound fracture of his collarbone.

Not more than a year later I participated in my second rodeo before a hometown crowd in Rochester. I entered the steer-wrestling event with a true sense of confidence. I knew the larger-framed cowboys were thinking deep down about how I wouldn't have a chance. I simply rationalized that what I lacked in size, I'd make up for with speed and determination.

Before a crowd of three thousand spectators, I, as the only local participant in steer-wrestling, threw my longhorn in six seconds. I won the event that night and will never forget the roar of the applause from the crowd or the blank stares from the other cowboys.

After spending nearly four long years at the University of Minnesota, I was at last in my final quarter. Before long, I realized the schooling, the dairy barn, and the rodeo would soon be mere history, and simply moments to remember.

I'd met many friends and gained exceptional experiences during my four-year absence from the family farm. Now, however, I was getting impatient for that farm and longed for the place in life where I knew I belonged.

17

○ ○ ○ ○

The Commencement of a New Horizon

"Gosh, Dad, it feels good to be home again," I said. "I don't ever want to leave the farm again."

"The family sure missed you while you were gone," Dad replied, "I have always dreamed of farming with my boys."

After all those years of hard work and hard schooling, I had finally graduated. Now I was back in my room in the house and content once again. My brother, Jerry, was married by this time and was living in another house on the farm. It certainly seemed exciting to imagine the accomplishments we could achieve with the three of us men pooling our resources for the farm.

No longer were Jerry and I simply helpers on the farm. We had finally become adults and were aiding Dad in the decision-making as well as the labor aspects of the farm.

Soon after returning home, I went to the local bank to apply for a loan. With the borrowed money, I invested in both the dairy and the beef enterprises on our farm. It seemed a little frightening to invest such large sums of money, with such large interest rates, knowing the money had to be paid back. This, however, was the only way farming could be accomplished. Farmers must work with tens of thousands of dollars the way most people work with hundreds of dollars.

Shortly after returning to the farm I received an interesting phone call. An agriculture teacher in the city of Rochester was on the line.

"Scott, this is Vern Bushlack. I've got a proposition for you."

"Yes, go ahead," I directed.

"You just recently graduated from the university with a double degree in animal science and agriculture education, is that correct?" he questioned.

"That's right," I replied.

"Did you attain a teaching certificate?" Vern asked.

"Well, I did, but I'm not planning on teaching, because I'm full-time farming with my brother and father," I returned.

For the remainder of the conversation, Vern explained he was in desperate need of another agriculture instructor for their program. Evidently several students had signed up for classes in production agriculture, forestry, and wildlife. He was confronted with either dropping many students out of the agriculture program or finding another teacher.

I once again informed him I was deeply sorry, but I just didn't feel I could help him out. I said good-bye, and then hung up.

For the next three weeks, I received a similar call from Vern about once a week. He desperately wanted my teaching services. Finally, I talked it over with my Dad and brother. We decided I should try the job, because it would certainly give me valuable experience. Dad and I felt the job could only be taken, though, if I signed a half-year contract. Under those arrangements, Vern would have enough time to select another instructor and still not be forced to drop students from any classes.

I offered my proposal to the school officials, and, before I knew what had happened, I was teaching high school students about agriculture.

Although my days were long and tiresome, I deeply enjoyed working with my students. Each day consisted of milking cows at five o'clock in the morning, doing chores, running to school to teach, then returning home again for the night chores and milking. Between all those items on my schedule, I had to find time for meetings, preparing lessons to teach, and working with students for judging team participation.

When my half-year contract had expired, the school found another instructor as my replacement, and I was allowed to peacefully get back to a farming routine. My teaching experiences were extremely rewarding, interesting, and fulfilling. I often like to think back and remember the students as well as the experiences we shared together.

By the time I had finally finished with all my extracurricular activities and was farming full time, I had reached the ripe old age of twenty-four years. At this point, one may ask what ever happened to my "love life." After all, my brother, Jerry, was happily married and farming. My folks were happily married and farming. My sister, Julie, was happily married to a deputy sheriff from an adjacent county, and they were doing a little farming on the side. All that remained unmarried were my younger sisters, Sally and Marcia, and I.

I had dated many girls while attending college. Likewise, I'd tried the courting process with several women after returning to the farm. I'd had some fun times and some bad times with girls that were veterinarian students, pharmacy students, animal-science students, teachers, and nurses. In many instances, I formed long-lasting friendships with many of the girls. In most cases, however, I could never find that one girl who shared many of my common interests and goals. That one deep and gratifying relationship with a member of the opposite sex kept eluding me. I will admit there were times when I questioned whether the right person actually existed.

Prior to my graduation from college, I stumbled across a most interesting girl. With only two months of schooling left, a new woman student had been hired to work in the research dairy barn. I saw her for the first time while working one day at the barn. Without hesitation, I asked the new girl what her name was. She informed me her name was Astrid Sammeli. For some tactless reason, I started laughing, and, with an honest attempt to be witty, I asked her if she was some kind of foreigner or something. She simply turned around and muttered, "What a creep!" under her breath as she walked away.

Hardly bothered by her actions, I set forth to find out the reason for her having been hired. It was a well-known fact at the barn that few female students were ever hired to milk cows. A few women had previously been hired, but normally the results didn't prove to be exceptional. Not only was the hour of three in the morning miserable for milking, but the physical side of the work was also difficult. The dairy barn had few automated machines that did the work. Most farms have automatic barn cleaners, pipeline milking systems, and silo unloaders. The research barn, however, had none of these conveniences. With them, very little student labor would have been needed.

I was never bothered whether guys or girls were milking and working at the barn as long as everyone pulled their own weight. What did bother me, though, was when a girl (this happened with some guys as well) was hired, and then she would never do the hard jobs. The reason was usually because something was too heavy or too difficult. Those attitudes invariably resulted in the other workers, including me, having to put in even harder hours during work.

I went directly to the boss and questioned him about the girl's qualifications. He informed me she had been a dairy princess in her county and had shown cattle at fairs. He further explained she had dairy farmed with her parents her entire life and was good at it. I remember walking away and thinking to myself, "We'll see if she's good at dairying in this barn!"

In the following days, I watched Astrid out of the corner of my eye. Surprisingly, she was good at the work. The cute, blond-haired girl could milk, clean pens, throw silage, and clip hair on the cows as well as anyone I'd ever seen work at the barn. For days I simply watched Astrid and spoke very little with her. Beyond my control, though, I found myself becoming attracted to her like a magnet.

Brian and I were cleaning the manure from a calf pen one day when I asked, "Brian, do you think that new girl, Astrid, would go out with me if I asked her?"

"If you don't ask her, I'm going to," he commented. "She looks like quite a gal to me."

Without further hesitation, I walked up to Astrid, who was trimming the hair on a cow. With my bib overalls covered with manure and my shirt drenched in perspiration, I asked her another simple and, once again, tactless question, "Do you have a boyfriend?"

Immediately I saw the what-a-creep look come over her eyes. I hated myself for having such a thick tongue. Fortunately, she noticed I was trying to be sincere, because at last she replied, "No, I don't have a steady boyfriend."

Sighing a breath of relief I asked, "Would you like to go to a movie and out to dinner tonight?"

After a brief pause Astrid said, "That sounds nice. Yes, I'd like to go with you."

I hurriedly ran back to the calf pen and shouted, "Brian, she said she'd go out with me!"

That night Astrid and I went to the movie, then to a restaurant for a bite to eat. The movie was a bit tense for both of us. She sat on the far side of her chair, and I on the far side of mine. I was much too tense to hold her hand or put my arm around her.

At the restaurant, we both loosened up somewhat. Astrid began telling me she was a junior working for an animal-science degree. After talking back and forth for a short time, I asked her, "What are you planning to do when you graduate from school?"

"I'm going back to my folks' farm, and start farming on my own," she calmly replied.

With that, I broke out in an all-out fit of laughter. I figured she must be kidding, so I said, "You mean, you're going to try and find a husband, then take over your parents' farm."

Astrid simply sat there staring blatantly at me. Finally I let my chuckles subside, as I began realizing she was not kidding.

Her what-a-creep look started flashing across her eyes once again, so I tried to break the tension and kiddingly asked, "Will you marry me?"

"No!" she almost shouted. "My folks are both in their mid-sixties, and I'm an only child. I don't want to fall in love with some guy and then get married before I go back to the farm. If that happened, my plans would probably have to be altered, and I don't want that."

I sat there in wide-eyed shock. This girl really meant what she had just said.

We sat there and continued the discussion for a while. I informed her that most guys would have sold their souls to marry a girl in her position. After all, getting into farming today is almost impossible without having the farm in one's family or marrying into a farm. I finally told her we wouldn't be able to marry anyway, because I had my farm I was going back to, and she had hers.

When the evening was over, I took Astrid back to her apartment. I walked her to the door, said good night, then left. As I drove away, I remember thinking some strange thoughts. I felt she probably hadn't really experienced a very enjoyable time, and I knew I'd had better dates.

With only a few weeks of college left prior to graduation, I spoke with Astrid at the barn on a few occasions, and we dated a couple of additional times. When the day of my graduation came, I said good-bye to my college friends, to the dairy barn, and to Astrid.

Days and weeks passed rapidly. My life on the farm seemed somehow similar to what life had been like in college. I was still milking cows and going to school, only this time I was being paid as a teacher, and not paying out as a student. I dated various girls when I had the time, but the end result was invariably the same. Where could I find someone to spend my life with that could love animals and love farming as I did? I knew the answer, but I couldn't figure out how to arrive at the solution.

Finally I called Astrid long distance in St. Paul one day and invited her to spend a weekend on my farm. At first she was hesitant, but at last she accepted my invitation. When we got together on the farm that weekend, something wonderful happened within us. It was as though we had been born in two separate parts of the universe, but fate had somehow forced our paths to cross. Astrid was everything I had ever dreamed about in a woman. She was beautiful, witty, a hard worker, and definitely a farmer.

The following weeks proved to be somewhat of a challenge. I had given up on dating all other girls and opted to develop a relationship with Astrid. Dad often kidded me about dating her. He often said, "You couldn't find a local girl, could you? You had to find someone who lives over a hundred miles away."

True it was; I was falling in love with this girl, and she with me. I soon found my whole world revolving around her very existence. She made the sun shine brighter in the morning and the grass grow greener in the meadows. I thought nothing of calling Astrid long distance and talking with her for an hour. Likewise, on any weekend I could chance to get away, I would hop in a car or on my motorcycle and visit her for a few hours in the city. It certainly was a challenge to date someone living a hundred miles away, but, with time, our love for each other grew and grew.

During Astrid's senior year of college, I asked her to marry me. Unlike the time I'd jokingly proposed in the restaurant during our first date, she gleefully accepted. With abounding happiness we prepared for our forthcoming marriage.

Much to Astrid's dismay, however, certain details had worked out in the opposite way she had hoped for. Astrid had sworn no man would come into her life and alter her plans of taking over her parents' farm. Years ago, she had promised her father to come back to the farm, then start dairying and cropping the farm on her own. As is often the case, a father works a lifetime to attain a farm, then generally wants his son or sons to carry on the family tradition. Since Astrid was her father's only hope, our forthcoming marriage shattered many dreams within her family.

Astrid and I discussed the dilemma many times with each other. No matter how we looked at the problem, it always ended up with her and me farming on my farm after she finished her schooling. I was in a position that was difficult to change or modify. After college, I bought into my family's farm operation as a partner and took a job as a teacher as well. At that point Astrid's only commitment to her family's farm was a verbal one. Her parents, difficult though it would be, would have to sell the farm so they could retire.

Astrid struggled severely with the decision, but finally agreed we had no other choice. After our wedding, we would take up residency on my farm in Byron.

A few months prior to the wedding, I drove up to St. Paul, picked up Astrid from school, and drove her and me to her parents' farm for a visit. The drive was a long one from my farm. To make the hundred-and-fifty-mile trip, I had to drive three tiresome hours.

Hilbert and Mildred were Astrid's parents, and their lifelong farm was located close to a small rural town called Kimball, Minnesota. St. Cloud was the largest city of substantial size in the area.

When Astrid and I arrived at the farm, we said hello to her parents and sat down for a talk. I cannot express the tension in the room that day. Hilbert asked point blank if I would consider farming on his farm. I informed him his daughter and I had given it much thought, but the chances weren't likely.

At that moment her father spoke words of true wisdom. Hilbert informed me that partnerships sometimes work and many times fail. He stated that since my Dad was only twenty years my senior, and, since my brother was in the partnership as well, a power struggle could surely emerge. Hilbert calmly said that, if Astrid and I were to take over his farm, he'd gladly step back, and we would be the sole operators.

I gave Astrid's father no answer at that time, and we finished out our visit conversing on other topics.

When I returned home to my farm later that day, I discussed Hilbert's proposal with my family. Dad and Jerry both expressed how it would be difficult to see me move away again so shortly after returning to the farm from college. If I moved this time, it would be far away and most likely permanent. I told my family to think about the problem for a few days before discussing their feelings.

Later that evening, after milking the cows, I strolled quietly around the farm in the soft moonlight. As I walked, I thought back to when I was a small, inquisitive boy. I remembered the farm as it had been years ago and how it was now. With the sweat from our bodies, Dad, Jerry, and I had built the farm up from a mere house with a few shacks, to a beautiful, modern farm. I leaned up against a fencepost and gazed out into the pasture. From the peaceful darkness of the pasture came the gurgling sounds of our creek, which had been such a part of my childhood. My mind drifted through memory upon memory. "Could I leave all this?" I asked myself. I loved the farm and loved my family immensely. If I moved far away to Astrid's farm, would I really be happy?

As I stood there motionless, I compared the two farms in my mind. Astrid's farm was older, more run down, had dilapidated fences, unpainted buildings, hilly farm land, and rocky soil. Dad's farm was completely the opposite in every respect. Still, Hilbert had certainly struck the right chord when he said Astrid and I would be the sole operators and owners. I'd dreamed for years of farming on my own and making my own decisions. A partnership with my father and brother had been my only choice, a choice which definitely gave me no problems, however. At last, I halted my mental torment and went to the house for some sleep.

A few days later, the family informed me they had discussed the issue. Dad repeated once again how much he had wanted both his boys farming with him. He then sadly commented that, since all three of us men had started drawing a living off the farm for our own families, the cash flow problems had started compiling. Our farm was too large for a one-family operation, yet the farm wasn't large enough to support three individual families.

My father sadly admitted that, if I had such a golden opportunity to start farming on my own with my future bride, I would certainly be foolish not to capitalize on it.

My family's feelings brought a lump in my throat, but, deep in my heart, I knew the decision was for the welfare of everyone involved.

A few months later Astrid and I were married on a blustery, snowy, but memorable day in March. Shortly after, I moved all my belongings from my family's farm to our new farm. My teaching contract had expired by then, so it posed no threat to my farming endeavor. I brought the animals I owned on Dad and Jerry's farm with me. By the time spring had fully arrived, I was relocated, and Astrid and I were ready for the commencement of a new horizon.

My beloved wife and I diligently labored together to make a respectable farming operation. We built new fences, repaired and painted buildings, tilled the soil, and filled our new farm with a vast array of animals.

The animal stories I've written about in this book are but a few of the many, many tales I grew up with dealing with animal life.

As I sit here writing my closing sentences, I look out over my own farm and see the makings of a multitude of future stories. Even now my dog, Trouble; our pig, Red; our cats, Wilma and Musta Black; Astrid's cow, Andrea; as well as the countless other animals on the farm are developing unique, exciting personalities.

I love my chosen life, which revolves around an infinite number of animal encounters. I'll forever be indebted to my nonhuman friends for helping to shape my life.

Epilogue

It's been nearly thirty years since I finished *The Folk and Their Fauna* in 1982. Over those years, my life has evolved in countless ways. Since the release of my first book, I've written and published a second book titled *Nine Lives To Eternity.* Several chapters of that book are also devoted to my lifelong involvement with many of God's creatures.

One constant throughout my existence has been that my love of animals has never waned. Today my wife Astrid and I still dwell on our multi-generational family farm as described in chapter seventeen. Each and everyday, my family and I are blessed to share some of our most cherished moments with a host of critters.

For instance, we have a flock of free-ranging hens that reward us with eggs for breakfast each morning. The hens scour our farm-site in search of insects to devour for a tasty meal. Our pesky rooster creates quite an irritation though, since he insists on positioning himself near the bedroom window and then begins crowing everyday well before the crack of dawn. I've always believed that the rooster's alarm clock is somehow improperly adjusted for a different time zone perhaps, because he always shatters the still of the night with his ear-splitting crow sometime around the wee-hour of 3:00 am. Each morning I contemplate just how good he might taste as a meal of fried chicken, and then I realize that I probably needed to arise for a middle of night bathroom visit anyway, so he is often forgiven for his audacity.

Joining our chickens is an array of other creatures such as ducks, geese, turkeys, mules, llamas, goats, cats, dairy cows, and our dog Rascal. Each animal has a unique personality and is such a blessing.

As three decades have passed since the release of this book, one could only imagine how shallow life would have been throughout the years without the influence of all the animals in our lives.

During our journey through life, my wife and I have been blessed with two fine sons, each of which was raised to love and appreciate animals much as we have. Our eldest son Trevor and his wife Theresa have a cherished relationship with their dog Smokey. Our youngest son Travis, his wife RaeLynn, and our granddaughter Hiltina have a wonderful relationship with their beloved dog Izzy. There is little doubt that both of our sons and their families will co-exist with a host of animals throughout their lives.

The Folk and Their Fauna meaning the people and their animals will hopefully bring you back to your own fond memories with a special creature.

Edwards Brothers,Inc!
Thorofare, NJ 08086
19 January, 2011
BA2011019